We are born snowflakes
Each different
We begin to melt
The day we are born...

When Magic Was Alive

The 1960's was a time of magic, an era very difficult to put into words. An era that had to be lived. Feelings are hard to put into words. Emotions felt with the heart are almost impossible to express with the pen.

I was a teenager in the 60's and a hippie (or flower child) in every sense of the word. To me being a hippie didn't mean just wearing elaborate costumes, smoking pot, and being free willed. It also meant being open to new adventures, ideas, people and above all music.

On Mondays, friends at my high school would come to class with tales of "Coke" dates, drive-in movies or beach parties. How could I explain that I had been to Hollywood, "The Strip" several blocks on Sunset Boulevard?

Walking into Bido Lido's, on Cosmos Street (a dark winding alley), listening to a new group called Love. Bido Lido's, with its low dark ceilings and brick walls, was exciting and daring in comparison.

Arthur Lee would lead his band into "Seven and Seven Is" or "Alone Again Or", and I was transformed. Everything melted away except the music.

Other nights, we would go to Pandora's Box and listen to music in the bright pink house setting on a triangle in the middle of an intersection. Later we would go outside and hang out with our Hollywood friends. Most of whom you would never bring home to meet your parents.

Everyone dressed in amazing costumes. I would spend hours in class, planning out what I was going to wear to Hollywood that weekend. Usually a very short mini dress with flowers, or different colored ribbons, in my hair and Twiggy style makeup, or lots of velvet and jewels, usually bought at the "Glass Farmhouse" in Silverlake. A beautiful shop filled with all kinds of amazing clothes and accessories.

The "Whiskey a Go Go" had groups like The Doors, Buffalo Springfield, and The Byrds. For us, it was an especially fun place to go. Not only because of the fantastic music but also because the manager Mario really liked us. Even though the line to get in would snake around the block, when Mario saw us, he would say loudly "My Nieces" as he motioned us ahead of everyone, some had been waiting for hours. We would hug him and walk in saying "Thank you Uncle Mario".

At 16 it made me feel like a celebrity. Once inside, it was dark and dank smelling with people sitting at tables. Jim Morrison sang, "Come on baby light my fire" as he danced and screamed himself across the stage. Standing there I never wanted to leave.

Capital Records on Sunset and Vine had glass record booths. You could sit and listen to the newest albums while looking out onto the street. Everyone always awaited the newest releases of our favorite groups. The covers to the albums were almost as incredible as the music. I would take the records home and play them repeatedly. When I'd finally take an album off the player one of my parents would yell from the other room, "Thank you." I'd think, "If only you knew." The music would always take me away. To this day no matter where I am when I hear certain songs, like the Moody Blues "Tuesday Afternoon", Love's "Alone Again Or", McArthur's Park, The End, even the Seeds "Pushin Too Hard", it always takes me back to that time of innocence, wonder, and love.

The Fifth Estate was another hangout that was unusual and exciting because you always felt so grown up there. When you went in, you'd order a coffee and a chocolate éclair then sit in one of the rooms with the overstuffed chairs. There were posters on the walls, some glowing, some not. You'd sit, chatting with everyone who was sitting or standing around.

Or you could go outside to the courtyard and mingle with everyone. It was so freeing standing outside under the stars with the soft Santa Anna winds blowing your hair. In the background you could hear Donavan's newest album playing

"The Sunshine Came Softly Through My Window Today". It was magical.

Although my parents would have fainted had they known I was in Hollywood every weekend (they always thought I was at a sleepover or bowling). It really was a very safe place to be. After all, it was a time of Love and Peace.

There was one night though, that was not so peaceful. That was the night of the riot at Pandora's Box. Police everywhere, some even on horseback. "Something's happening here" and it wasn't good. The kids were upset and frightened. Because we were always peaceful and fun loving, we couldn't understand why the police were making it into something it wasn't. "There's a man with a gun over there, telling me you've got to beware."

Of course, everyone scattered. My friends and I ran to Swabs. The night went on with police confronting kids. I headed home wondering how this event was going to affect our places on "our strip". Not long after that they tore down Pandora's Box. Now, only a cement triangle remains.

After a night of walking up and down the strip visiting with people we knew and meeting new ones, we'd all head to Canter's at 2:00 a.m., but never before 2:00. It was always very crowded, and we'd wait for a booth. So many kids both inside and out. When we got a booth, we'd have a bagel and a Coke, or a black and white cookie.

We'd hang out for a while and then go to a friend's house (always older who had their own apartment) and spend the night sleeping on the floor. Staying up until dawn talking, smoking joints, and listening to records. Always very innocent.

One night, while standing outside of Canter's, I met this girl. We started talking (little did I know then that we would become lifelong friends). I told her that we had been invited to go over to these guys house to listen to an album they had just recorded.

She said, "Well no thanks"; she "Didn't do that." I guess she assumed we were going to their house to spend the night with them. I said "Oh no, it's not like that, we don't' do that either. We're just going to listen to music". Sounds super naïve now, but we all went. The guys could not have been nicer or more gentlemanly. Weeks later their newly recorded album was soaring off the charts. You could not go anywhere without hearing " In-A-Gadda-Da-Vida" by Iron Butterfly. It was such an honor to have been one of the first to hear it.

Life has a way of moving along. Waiting around the corner for me was travel to the UK, Europe, time in New York, college, and later marriage and three amazing daughters.

I have always felt that my daughters are fortunate indeed to have a Hippie for a mother. I was and always will be a Hippie/Flower Child at heart.

I raised my daughters to be colorblind, free thinking, and respectful of others without judging. Who knows what someone else has been through or is going through to make them the way they are.

I still bake our bread, make my own granola, and I raised them all to be vegetarians, despite a non-vegetarian Father. I have always tried to instill in my daughters, that it's the little things that make up this thing called Life.

Today a lot of people are starting to think about Mother Earth. I'm glad to see that, but I remind my daughters that we "Hippies" started caring for Her way back in the 60's with communes, recycling, and in general trying to get back in tune with nature.

I guess everything comes full circle. My feelings, emotions, concerning the 60's are so close to my heart that they totally make up who I am today. I wouldn't trade being a teenager in the 60's for anything.

I know I will always be thankful for being a "Hippie".

I meant to do my work today
but the fragrance of the freesia's
kept pulling me away...

In the day of surfers, hodads, nerds, and all the people who just went along in life, we "Hippies" soaked everything up like a sponge. That sponge still seeps into every facet of my life, for which I am forever grateful...

It's Hard to Hide Invisible Scars

To this day, she never wears fingernail polish. Sometimes, when she's going away to the shore and her daughters insist, she'll wear a pale pink color on her toes—but never her fingers. The reason for this is a nun.

She grew up on Long Island. Her family was not a tight knit one, she was mostly raised by maids. During the Winter months, her parents always went to Florida to meet up with their group of friends. It was the fashion back then, getting away from the cold and snow and meeting up with friends in sunny Florida. Her parents always left her and her older sister with a Nanny. The Nanny had to be an R.N. She guessed it gave them peace of mind. Knowing that if something should occur, she and her sister would be in good hands.

She was used to being left on her own. Social obligations kept her parents busy. She rarely spoke to her sister. She didn't like this way of living, in fact she hated it. She wanted a real family, a family that was close, and united. Everyone envied her. They would have thought her ungrateful to want more. Considering all she had, she didn't want more things. She would gladly have traded her stately home, maids, toys, and beautiful clothes to have a close family.

A family that sat around the dinner table at night and talked over the day's events and asked what had happened at school that day, or what she did at recess. A family with someone to tuck her into bed at night and listen to her hopes and dreams.

Inside she was always on guard, on guard to be the perfect child, never a problem to her parents. She knew that when they returned from Florida laden with gifts, they would ask how everything had gone in their absence. She never went into much detail. After all, the questions were just an obligation.

One night after dinner the Nanny motioned her over to display fingernails painted a bright red. The Nanny then insisted on painting her fingernails the same bright red. Once painted, she hated them, red droplets of blood on each finger. But she smiled and thanked the Nanny before she went up to bed.

She attended a private parochial school. In class the next morning, Sister Mary Marie had decided to have an oral pop quiz on multiplication. Multiplication was something she was not very good at (except of course the 2's, 5's, 10's and 11's). Sister Mary Marie called on her to answer 8 times 9. She sat there trying to do it in her head but wasn't quick enough.

Sister walked slowly, black lace-up shoes clicking on the wooden floors, then stopped at her desk. Sister Mary Marie was in a foul mood. The long black gown and veil with bleached white muslin taught across the forehead. The heavy rosary hung from Sister's middle. Jesus hanging on the large wooden cross dragging almost to the floor.

She sat there terrified at being singled out. All eyes of her classmates on her—some sympathetic some not. The wooden ruler swaying back and forth before her eyes like a metronome. She could not come up with the correct answer and was afraid to say an incorrect one.

Looking up she was about to say, "I'm sorry Sister. I don't know the answer." It was then Sister Mary Marie noticed her fingernails. The look that crossed Sister's face chilled her to the bone.

Sister Mary Marie said, "Well, if you had time to paint yourself up, you had time to learn your multiplication tables! Write them thirty times each as a punishment tonight."

She wanted to say that she hadn't painted her nails. She hated the way they looked. She wished she could remove the color right now, right this minute. But instead she said, "Yes Sister."

At recess some of the girls, her friends, came over to her and said that they thought her nails looked pretty. She had been trying to chip the polish off with her other nails and her teeth. She didn't show them and only said, "Thank you."

That night she asked the Nanny to remove the polish. Saying that it had chipped at recess. The Nanny asked, "Would you like me to repaint them a different color?"

"No, thank you," was all she said as she held out her hands...

Dear Two Two:

Personally, I think you spend too much time listening
to worn out records.
Who cares, if you know all the words? They're not
yours.
Now is the time to stop singing.
Girls make better lovers than heroes.
See you at the Rugby match.
I'll be the one waving the Polish flag.

Just so you'll know
Your Pen Pal
~Queenie

Mr. Leonard

Mr. Leonard died in his sleep. Peacefully, just as he had lived his life. Mrs. Leonard went to wake him for breakfast and found him cold and unresponsive. He looked pale blue. She stood frozen. She had never seen a dead person before. Now she was looking at the lifeless figure of her husband. John looked at peace, calm, almost boyish once again. He had a slight curl to his lips. Making him look as though he were smiling at her. The way he always did, when he wanted to surprise her with something, or if he knew she was upset. It was his way of winning her over.

She didn't remember how long she stood by his side of the bed looking at him. Suddenly it hit her that he was gone. Her John was dead. Where had the sixty-one years gone? Just yesterday they had stood side by side at the altar. Vowing to love each other forever, till death do them part. Now that death had parted them, she wasn't sure what to do. Surely, she should call someone. This was the kind of thing that John always handled, telling her not to fret. But fretting she was. Closing the door behind her, she walked slowly down the stairs and picked up the phone.

It felt like seconds before people were knocking at her door. She remembered she still had the phone in her hand when she went to answer the door. The fire department was asking to be let in. They asked her where Mr. Leonard was. She pointed upstairs and told them it was the second door to the right.

One of the lady firefighters took her by the arm and led her into the living room. She sat down on John's favorite chair, the one with the view of the garden. He would sit for hours watching the birds. They both enjoyed the coming and going of the many different birds. It was John who always made sure they were fed twice daily and the two birdbaths clean and full.

She sat in John's chair for what seemed like days. Staring stupidly out the window, the birds lighting on the feeders, feeders needing seed. A voice spoke to her. It was the fire chief saying he was sorry, but Mr. Leonard was gone. Such a kind man to speak to her so gently. Out of the corner of her eye she saw a stretcher being carried down the staircase. A lone figure, wrapped all in white, was strapped firmly to it. With a quick intake of breath, she said to herself, "Goodbye John."

She was asked if there was someone she wanted called. Mrs. Leonard looked at the lady firefighter as though she had just sprung up next to her chair like a mushroom after a spring rain and answered, "No, no there is no one to call. Only John," then quickly thought, "Now no one." She was as alone as one could be, no family. They had never been fortunate enough to have children. Though they both had longed for them. They just never came. She and John had faced the days and nights alone together. After a while it had seemed enough. They had their routine and they were satisfied with their life.

John had worked at the Post Office in the mailroom. He was always busy. Even though he was well liked by everyone, he never developed any friendships. He was happy to come home to her, his wife, and their simple carefree life. She was happy to keep house, try new recipes, and always have the house just right when John came home. They would have a glass of wine or sherry and chat about the events of the day before they had dinner. Then they laughed and planned the weeks ahead.

It had been the bits and pieces that formed their lives, nothing special and yet how very special. Funny how it's always the little things that make up the whole. All the special days, the holidays, were just a part of the large picture, the events that framed their lives.

The weeks after the earth swallowed John, she slowly moved through days that turned into nights. The constant tickling of the clock made her feel anxious. Was her time running out? She honestly didn't care. One day she climbed on the kitchen stool and took the clock down, removing its batteries. The endless ticking stopped. She did not need a clock to tell her that her days were numbered. A peace settled over her, and the house.

The first thing she did, when she began to feel like her old self, was to remember the birds. How long had they waited? Would they come back? Wrapping up against the cold north wind of November, she took out birdseed and suet and made sure the birdbaths were full of fresh water. When she came in, she made a pot of tea and sat down at the kitchen table. Truth be told, the walk to the bird feeders had tired her. She had been spending most days reading and only eating what she must.

She sat there thinking about Thanksgiving (a holiday she and John had celebrated). It was almost here. She wondered, for what did she have to be thankful

Finally, out of necessity, she forced herself to dress and walk to the shops. She had begun to realize that no matter how much she dreaded the dawning of each new day; dawn still broke the night.

The shops were full. The holidays were almost here, and everyone was scurrying about to get what they needed. She thought maybe she should buy a small turkey or chicken and roast it. She was trying to be merry, but her heart just wouldn't permit it, so soon. No one spoke to her. She purchased only necessities. Tea, milk, sugar, bread, eggs, nothing special, just what she'd use daily.

She began the slow trip home. How terrible it was to walk into an empty house. Knowing that no one was there. She put her groceries away and made a cup of tea. After finishing her tea, she decided to go out and take care of the birds. "John would be pleased," she thought as she filled each feeder, the wind biting her cheeks. It gave her peace to know that she was caring for their birds.

As quickly as an autumn leaf falling, it was almost Christmas. A beautiful snow had fallen the night before and she awoke to a vast whiteness that filled her with joy and wonder. For the first time, since John had left her, she felt hopeful. Not happy but not quite so sad either. She turned on the radio and listened to Christmas carols as she made her oatmeal. While finishing her tea, she decided to put up their tree. She quickly set her cup down and went to the Christmas closet. Inside were all the decorations and special ornaments they had collected over the years. Each one a treasure, each one a voice whispering into her ear the story it had to tell.

They had a small tree with the lights already on. She put it on the table by the fireplace where it had always stood and put the red plaid skirt around its bottom. She sat down to gaze at it from John's chair. It warmed the room. She could almost hear John saying how lovely it was, as he always did. She sat there for a long time, thinking. When the sky turned a kaleidoscope of colors, she went out to feed their birds.

Coming in, she glanced at the tree and thought, "There are no presents. There should be presents under a tree." It was her first Christmas without John to buy presents for her.

After sitting by the fire and looking at their tree, the memories of all their long-ago Christmas's filled her with warmth. She hadn't felt like that since John left. It was almost like he was sitting next to her sharing their stories, some old, some new. She suddenly felt an obligation to carry on their traditions. It was then she made up her mind. Tomorrow she would walk into town and pick up things she needed for Christmas Eve and Christmas Morning. The things she always bought. She would cook all the things she used to cook, to make the days special.

It was with a serene feeling that she heated the water for her hot water bottle that night. As she carried it to bed, she was humming, "Come All Ye Faithful", one of her favorites since she was a little girl.

How different she felt in the morning when she opened her eyes. She was going to town not to shop for necessities but to keep their Christmas. The house would be filled with the scents of their Christmas's Past.

As she prepared her breakfast she was smiling, knowing John would be pleased and proud of her for being brave and carrying on. She tidied up the house and then wrapped herself up warmly. It had lightly snowed last night, so white and clean. She could hardly wait to step out on the untouched canvas. Making her way into town, carefully lest she slip and fall, she felt renewed. Her sorrow was still great and sometimes hit her when she least expected it. A certain smell or a creak on the stairs and she'd catch herself about to say, "John is that you?" Then the tears would flow and that dreadful morning of finding him in bed would hit her like a slap to the face.

The little village was crowded with people buying last minute gifts and special items to cook for the holiday. She went from one store to the next buying what she needed. In some stores, she brought things she wanted, more than needed. Shortbread cookies, besides the tins were so pretty, Scottie dogs with bright red bows on their necks.

She thought she'd stop at the tearoom and have a cuppa, with maybe a scone, before she started the long walk home. The shops had been very nice as always and offered to bring her purchases to her, which she gladly accepted. Too much fresh snow and ice underneath to carry them herself.

The tearoom was warm and cozy. She enjoyed looking out the window as she sipped her tea. A lady came in carrying a large bundle of shiny wrapped presents. Suddenly she was reminded of their little tree at home with nothing except the plaid skirt under its branches. She thought maybe she'd buy something for herself and put it under the tree. She'd have a present to open on Christmas morning. She could pretend it was from John. Then she thought, "No, best not go there." A wonderful meal and a fire in the fireplace while Christmas carols played would be gift enough. Yet her eyes kept going back to those beautiful boxes.

The waitress came and asked if she'd like more tea. She answered, "No, thank you" and said, "I must be going, so much to do." While waiting for her check, she suddenly had the most wonderful idea. She quickly gathered up her purse and the few small boxes she was carrying and left the shop.

Once outside she walked to a bench in front of her favorite little gift ship. The one where John always shopped for her. She sat there waiting. She knew she'd know whom to choose. After about ten minutes, a young woman, maybe in her late twenties, walked up to the shop. She stood up from the bench, and called to her saying, "Excuse me Miss, may I please speak with you for a moment?"

The young lady was very pretty with long auburn hair and sharp green eyes. She had a quick smile. Her cheeks were rose pink from the cold as she said, "Yes?"

Quickly introducing herself (not without a few tears) she explained the situation to the young woman, who introduced herself as Carol. Giving Carol ten pounds she told her to spend it all. To choose something she would like to have, something beautiful. Carol gave her a quick hug and said she'd be back in a bit.

She walked back to the bench and sat down to wait. It seemed like a long time, but she enjoyed being out. She felt connected with the people trying to finish before the shops closed.

She had become so engrossed with watching a mother trying to get her two small sons off the merry-go-round in front of the greengrocers the she didn't notice Carol, had returned.

Smiling, Carol handed her the box and said, "I hope you will be pleased. They have so many beautiful things. It was hard to choose."

She stood to take the box. Thanking Carol, she tried to offer money for her time. Carol said, "No, of course not, I enjoyed doing it." Giving her a quick hug, she said, "Merry Christmas" and walked quickly back into the shop.

The box weighed more than a box that size should, she thought. She wondered what could be inside, as she walked home. Once there, she was about to look at the box again, when the door buzzer rang. It was her groceries. "So many packages just for me", she thought as she handed the man a generous tip. Thanking her he closed the door to her "Merry Christmas" wish.

She put away most of her purchases leaving out only what she needed to prepare for dinner and Christmas breakfast. She walked into the living room and started a fire in the fireplace then tuned the radio to Christmas carols. She felt excited. After all Christmas was to be celebrated and it was exactly what John would have wanted her to do.

She went to the bag that held her present, her only gift. Taking it out of the bag, she smiled at how beautifully it was wrapped. Very pale green paper with dark green sprigs of holly. It was tied with red ribbon, and a big bright red bow on the top. She carefully shook it, like she had done as a child, and then put it under the tree. It looked nice there, very Christmassy. She went to the kitchen to start on dinner and her breakfast. First, she made a cup of tea, humming as she began her tasks.

Christmas Eve dinner was delicious. She enjoyed sitting at the dining room table again with the candles lit. She tidied up and then went up to bed. Pulling down the shade she noticed it had started snowing again, a perfect end to such a lovely day. Her last thought, before she drifted off, was about Carol. Such a sweet young woman. So, understanding, maybe she knew the pain of a loss too. She hoped not.

Christmas morning dawned clear with a very weak sun shining on white as far as the eye could see. She dressed and headed downstairs to light a fire and heat breakfast. Once again turning on the tree and the radio.

With breakfast in the oven and a cup of tea in hand, she went to the tree and the warmth of the fire. Sitting in John's chair, she took the box and put it on the small table next to her. As she did, a card she had not noticed the day before slipped onto the floor. Picking it up, she opened the red envelope. Inside a card with a shining church covered with snow read, "Merry Christmas and all good things in the New Year." Underneath the printed greeting was a handwritten note saying, "I wish you a Merry Christmas and I also wish to be your friend. Please call me. We should get to know one another." It was signed, "Your friend, Carol," with her number.

She was touched, how sweet, how lovely to have a friend. She would call her. She did want to get to know her better and maybe her family too.

Being careful not to rip the paper, she gently opened the box. Inside was a brown cardboard box with a star sticker holding it closed. When she opened the lid, a small gasp escaped her lips. Inside the box was the most beautiful snow globe she had ever seen. Its glass held two small cardinals perched on a branch. It didn't play a song. When turned upside down and then righted snow fell so heavily that you could not see the birds until the snow slowly settled. The two birds' beaks, almost touching, seemed oblivious to the snow and continued to look at each other as the snow fell silently around them.

What a gift, what a treasure. It was as if Carol had known their love of birds. John would have loved this gift. She could not have found a better present if she had bought it herself. Looking at it she felt a warmth wrap around her. She felt safe, cozy, and at peace. She felt John...

I'm still taking care of my body
Since you went away

I still wash my hair with rain shampoo
Sometimes it curls
The way you liked

I find myself wishing that you were here
To see and to touch it

I still wash with almond soap
The one you liked
For the fragrance it left

But none of the others
Who now touch my body
Ever seem to notice

I'm still taking care of my body
Which is only right I suppose

Only now
It seems
To matter so little...

The Delay

We were waiting in the International section of DFW Airport, when a loud voice announced the flight to Edinburgh Scotland had been changed to Frankfurt Germany.

Instead of being dismayed we were excited. Another stamp in our passport! We telephoned a few family members and friends, then boarded the plane that would now be taking us to Germany with Scotland in our near future.

The trip was uneventful, as most flights are. Exciting at first. Then, just boring. We wanted to see new things, meet new people, and experience new adventures.

I had been to my Scotland and Europe many times, but this was my first time traveling with my middle daughter. We were both looking forward to it. We both needed, wanted, a break.

On arriving in Frankfurt, it was plain to see that they were having one of the worst snowstorms in decades. Looking out the enormous window at all the planes on the tarmac, snow quickly engulfing them in white blankets, we realized we might be there a day or two.

The flight to Edinburgh had been cancelled. We soon learned that all flights were canceled and that we could be spending that night, maybe more, in the airport. After checking with several information counters, it became more and more evident that we would be sleeping in the airport indefinitely. We decided to look for a hotel.

We made a few phone calls on our own. Then we got a call from a friend back in the states, who had been calling every hotel in Frankfurt. He had found what surely must have been the last room in the city and had booked it for us.

We were elated that we wouldn't be spending the night on a plastic bench with all the other suddenly homeless. We went out to queue up at the taxi stand, with others who had managed to find lodging. The snow was falling heavily now

The taxi stand was full to overflowing. An elderly gentleman offered his umbrella to us, but I had a hood on my coat and my daughter had a scarf. Thanking him we declined it and continued standing in the snow.

Soon a taxi pulled up. We handed him the paper that had the name of the hotel. After a few blocks we got on the autobahn. Although it was difficult to see out the windows, the snow almost to a blizzard by now, it did seem that we were getting very far away from the airport.

I briefly wondered if the driver had understood the hotel location. About ten minutes later we were pulling down a road that had an almost alley like feel to it. The streetlights casting a dull yellow glow on the snow below. I had an uneasy, almost eerie, feeling. Because I felt we were in a somewhat desperate situation, the taxi already disappearing into the mist. It's taillights blinking red.

We went into a hotel only in the loosest term of the word. It seemed more like a hostel or the dorm of an inexpensive college, plain to the point of restrained. The man behind the front desk looked surly. While signing in, he showed none of the friendly mannerisms a hotel clerk usually displays. We took our key and headed to the fourth floor. I wanted nothing more than a warm shower, and to sleep. It had been a long, strange day.

On the way up in the tiny elevator, I noticed a lot of men in their early 20's just standing around talking in small groups. Never taking their eyes off us. We did not see another woman.

Once inside our room we were taken aback by the sparse accommodations. Two twin beds, one small dresser complete with lamp and phone. Two very large windows with sheer curtains no blinds or shades to afford privacy. We could see directly into the building across the narrow street.

Knowing all our clothes were on the plane, I immediately washed my underwear and socks, in the small sink provided. While washing them I could hear men, several, talking in a different language not German. Although I did not understand what they were saying, I did hear the word "girls" a few times. It was becoming obvious to me that this was not a good place to stay.

While my daughter was in the shower, I went to pull the chest in front of the door to be on the safe side. It was then I noticed the door opened outwards. I had never been in a hotel where the door opened out. I could hear men whispering in the hall right outside our door.

I went to the phone. I was going to call a taxi and have one waiting when my daughter got out of the shower. The deskman said, "Sorry you may receive calls, but you cannot make calls."

I thought, "That's it!" I knocked, pounded, on the bathroom door. My daughter came out with her head a snowball of shampoo. She seemed annoyed. I told her, "Get out. Get dressed. We're leaving." She started to ask questions but something on my face must have said, "Just do it!" She closed the door.

I sat on the bed trying to pull on soaking wet underwear and socks. The second I sat on the bed I felt this presence. I will always believe it was God's voice that audibly said, "Get out." Not in a menacing way, but in a hurry you've no time to lose way.

I felt an urgent need to leave. I again knocked on the bathroom door and in an insistent voice told my daughter to "Come out now!"

Pulling on wet knee socks is almost impossible but I had them on, half up but on. I had us packed and ready to walk out the door when my daughter emerged from the bathroom.

She asked, "May I ask what we're doing." I all but tossed her things at her and said, "We're leaving" as I headed to the door. She followed. In the hall were three young men but we were not accosted.

The man behind the desk asked if we were leaving. My daughter and I noticed that he was dialing the same number over and over becoming more anxious, almost frantic, with each new failed attempt. I said, "Yes" and never looked back.

It was difficult walking in knee-deep snow with wet underwear and socks. My feet were frozen by the time we got to the next hotel down the street. Walking in, we asked them to call us a taxi and they refused. We left and tried another place four doors down, they too said no. By now, I was becoming very concerned. There seemed to be no way out.

The street was dirty with trashcans overflowing. The streetlights gave off only the dimmest of light. The entire area had an ominous feel to it, forbidding and sinister.

We walked into the third place, a small dark hotel. This time I did not ask them to please call us a taxi. Instead, I said, "I am an American. Call us a taxi." The man behind the desk said he would but kept urging us to wait in the back room. He picked up the phone and called a taxi. Turning to me he said, "It's on its way. Come and wait for it in this room in the back."

We said, "No" and went to a small table by the window, where we could see the street, and waited. Within ten minutes a small white taxi pulled up in front. I told my daughter, "Come on" and in an instant we were inside. I quickly checked the drivers face with the one displayed on the visor above the passenger seat. We told him, "The airport please" I looked out the window as we drove away.

A feeling of indescribable relief came over me. I settled in watching the snow continuing to fall on this nightmarish night. Our driver (a young Italian man) said, "Do you mind if I ask you a question?" We had been making small talk. He was so refreshing compared to where we had just been. I said, "No, of course not." He said, "Well you seem like nice ladies. What were you doing in that part of town?"

I asked, "What do you mean?" The driver said, "That is a very dangerous part of town known for drugs, prostitution, and trafficking." I felt a cold chill run through my entire body. We had been two of the lucky ones. Two who had escaped. Perhaps just in time. We will never know for sure.

I have always believed in listening to what my instinct tells me to do. Now, more than ever, when I have a feeling about something, I follow it.

Quickly...

Billie

The days drift by unchanged
Flowing
One into another
Calm
Almost peaceful

Mornings open to day's events
Tasks to be accomplished
Fading into nights of slumber
Filled with dreams
Some good
Some not

Each day everyone carries on
No different on the outside
So changed on the inside
The time spent pushing feelings down
Holding them in
Could fill an ocean...

The Empty Jar

"When human hearts break and human hearts despair, then from the twilight of the past the great conquerors of distress and care, of disgrace and misery, of spiritual slavery and physical compulsion, look down on them and hold out their eternal hands to the despairing mortals."

~Adolf Hitler

September 1, 1939

Poland never had a chance.

Hitler sent out the command to kill without pity or mercy all men, women and children of Polish descent or language. He needed the space.

October 8, 1939

Polish Jews and non-Jews were stripped of all rights and subject to special legislation. Food and medicine were quickly gone.

1)   Young men were forced into German Army
2)   Polish language forbidden
3)   Schools and colleges closed
4)   Polish art and culture destroyed
5)   Polish churches and synagogues burned
6)   Polish cities and towns renamed in German
7)   Obliteration of all traces of Polish history and culture

Many Poles buried their belongings in their land. Hoping to return for it one day. Others hid theirs in walls and under floorboards, anywhere, to save their precious possessions from falling into the hands of the devil.

Your 16th birthday, what could be more special, more sacred, more "your" day.

Jozef had been looking forward to this incredible day for weeks. Shrugging off questions of what he wanted from his siblings as well as his mother and father. He knew what some of his four siblings would be giving (making for) him. As far as the gift from his parents, he didn't even dare to hope that what he longed for, could be given to him. Maybe on his 18th birthday he kept consoling himself. For turning 16, it was just too much to wish for.

The engraved gold pocket watch had been in his family for as far back as he could remember. His dad always carried it on the long gold chain, even when working in the garden. Its edges smooth with the constant checking of time. The passing of one's life, kept by an intricate gold timepiece. After a quick glance, his father would close the case. Putting it safely back into his warm pocket until he once again needed the assurance of time.

His dad had received it on his 18th birthday from his father. Who had been given it on his birthday and on and on since the beginning of the family. He knew someday this beautiful piece, this heirloom, would be his. He would just have to wait until his parents felt the time had come.

Until then he would admire the striking gold case, smooth as the breast of a dove. Marvel, at the efficient way it snapped open when you pressed the miniscule knob, raised just slightly above the smooth case. Revealing the stark white face with flat black Roman numerals and graceful almost ballet like hands that moved ever so slowly to count off the minutes.

Jozef had held this gem, this piece of history, in his hand's many times. Each time he took it into his own hands it gave him a pleasure that was impossible to describe. It had to be felt. He thought he could almost feel all the grandfathers, great grandfathers and on and on who had also held this timepiece and counted on it for its dependable faithfulness. Yes, to have this in the family was a fine thing. To know that someday it would be held in his hands as his own was something he looked forward to, the passing of time.

The sun felt warm on Jozef's eyes. He kept them closed; languishing in the comfort it gave. Today he was a man. Today he turned 16. A day to be remembered always, the corner turned, no looking back. The journey had brought him to this day, the end of childhood.

He could hear Mama downstairs in the kitchen scurrying about making his birthday breakfast. Papa and the others would be outside doing the chores. He was excused from chores today, family tradition on birthdays only.

He stretched and snuggled once again into his down comforter. Relishing both his day of leisure and the knowledge that when he did go downstairs it would be to a warm kitchen filled with Mama's delicious special treats. The smell of bacon mingling with fresh poppy seed rolls, is what finally had him up, dressed, and down the stairs.

Mama stood over the old black stove stirring something but quickly came to him with open arms. A long hug and a "Happy Birthday" kiss on the cheek. Standing back, she said, "An image of your Papa at 16 you are, and I should know. He was 16 when we began courting. Sit down and I'll give you a cup of coffee. The others will be finished soon."

Jozef sat down at his usual seat as Mama set a cup of strong black coffee in front of him. He could smell it as it sat on the table, dark and rich. "Smelling of earth and home," he thought, as he spooned sugar and stirred cream into the cup.

He noticed Mama had set the table with one of her best tablecloths. In the center of the table was a large canning jar full of wildflowers. It held an impossibly big assortment of wine cups, daisies, buttercups, and several tall dark green spears of grass all vying for room in the old jar. A gift no doubt from Anna, his youngest sister, who must have picked them early this morning while helping Bridget to gather the eggs.

Minutes later a not so cheery Adeline stomped in. Heading straight to the sink saying she was glad Jozef only had one birthday a year as milking cows was man's work. Once her hands had been washed, she took her seat at the table. Smiled and said, "Happy Birthday" as she handed Jozef a long thin box from her apron pocket. Saying, "Go ahead and open it.

He said, "Thank you" as he slid the top off. Inside was a beautiful pen, a blue ink pen, lying on a stark white piece of cotton.

Jozef was very pleased. He took it out to admire it more closely. Adeline said she had been noticing him looking at it for weeks now at John Dee's shop. She figured that was as good a clue as any as to what he'd like. He thanked her saying indeed he had been looking at it and thinking what a fine pen it was. He was very happy to call it his and to use it at school and at home. He tucked it safely into his shirt pocket making sure the side holder caught his shirt. He gave it a quick pat just to be sure.

Papa came in the back door saying, "Happy Birthday Son," as he went to the sink to wash his hands. Jozef knew he had been out milking. Mama was setting plates on to the table filled with eggs, bacon, potatoes and her delicious poppy seed rolls. Plates were passed around, till everyone had been served.

Jozef was on his second poppy seed roll when Bridget and Anna presented him with their present. Together they had tied a round object up in a piece of paisley material Mama had given them. He knew what it was before starting the long process of untying the string. But he managed to have his face register surprise and delight as he uncovered a new ball. A bright red one that, according to Bridget, had a lot of bounce. Jozef said it was a wonderful gift and he would give it a try right after breakfast. Anna said, "You can see the red really good in the grass."

Jozef was so happy to be spending this special day with the ones he loved most. Breakfast was delicious. No one in the world made poppy seed rolls like Mama, the crust so soft and just a bit chewy with the seeds making popping sounds in his mouth.

After the plates had been cleared, the girls laughing and pushing one another at the sink while Mama pretended to scold, everyone came back to the table. J.D. presented Jozef with his gift, two notebooks. J.D. said he noticed that Jozef had been writing a lot as of late and he felt the notebooks would come in handy.

One was covered in red cloth, the other in blue. Inside were endless pages just waiting to be filled with Jozef's thoughts, dreams and ideas. Adeline said, "You can use them with your new pen."

Jozef thanked J.D. and said, "Yes, these are just what I wanted." J.D. smiled with pleased satisfaction at having made a good choice.

Jozef looked around the table and thanked everyone for their gifts and Mama for the wonderful breakfast. It was then that Papa said, "Well, one more to open Son," as he handed him a lumpy handkerchief tied with a bow he recognized as one of Anna's hair ribbons. As he reached across the table to take it into his hand, he noticed his father's hand slightly trembled.
At once he knew the contents of the package. It was the watch! He knew it as sure as if it had not been wrapped at all. He felt it through the material, and he felt its weight.

Slowly he untied the ribbon and peeled away the handkerchief as though he were peeling an orange. There it was. Gleaming in the sunlight, a flame of gold in his hands, a piece of history, of family, of Poland. He was almost afraid to look into his father's eyes.

Now that it had been given to him, he suddenly felt unworthy. It felt too soon. How could Papa part with it? How would he tell time? How would he feel not seeing Papa take it out of his pocket several times a day? A final check at night before bed when he snapped it closed for the day. Knowing it would be waiting for him in the morning.

Minutes passed. Finally, Mama said, "Son are you pleased?"

Looking into her eyes, he-said, "Yes, very" then added, "But Papa so soon? What will you use?"

Papa said, "When I need to know the time, I will ask my Son."

Jozef was out of his seat embracing his Papa and promising him he would care for it always. Standing with his arms around Papa he said to the family, "Thank you, this is the best day of my life." The kitchen was a warm blanket, Jozef felt wrapped in love.

How impossible, how insane, to think that just three months later he and Papa would be putting this golden heirloom deep into the earth. Far down where it would not shine. Would not mark time. Would not have its smooth edges caressed. Instead it would lie dormant for years until a new owner would take possession of their home.

There was talk in the village. Papa said there would always be talk, too much talk, not enough work. Mama said nothing, but Jozef noticed dark circles under her leaf green eyes. There were days he would walk into the kitchen and find her standing in front of the sink, her mind a million miles away, as the kettle continued to whine and whine. When he'd gently say, "Mama?" she would jump with a start and say, "Oh my, oh my, the kettle!" Then she would walk to the stove and pour the boiling water into the teapot.

Jozef had mentioned this to Papa one evening as they forked hay into the wagon. Papa had looked at the sun setting for several minutes before he said, "Walk with me Son." He put his pitchfork against the wagon and started off towards the lane. Jozef felt frightened as he caught up with Papa. Papa put his arm around Jozef's thin shoulder and sighed a long deep sigh. Finally, he said, "Son, there is a madman amongst us. There is talk he will be here soon. On our soil, our Polish soil. He wants to take our land. He wants to take our country, our Poland."

Jozef said, "Who is this man Papa?"

Papa took a deep breath, looked directly into his son's eyes and said, "Son, his name is Hitler and he is the devil come to life. The villagers are afraid. I too Son, am afraid for all of us. That is why we must prepare."

"Prepare for what Papa? What must we do?"

Papa replied, "We must take all that we hold dear, all that is precious to us and hide it."

"But where do we hide such things Papa?"

"We will take our jewelry, little that we have, what money that we have and seal it tight into jars and bury it on our land Son. If we must leave our home, we will remember where it is, and come back for it one day. It will be our underground bank," said Papa as he began to laugh. Looking up at him in the failing light Jozef saw his face was wet with tears.

That night Jozef was woken up by a gentle push on his shoulder. His father stood next to his bed with the lantern on dim and told him to get up and get dressed quickly and to meet him in the kitchen. He did as he was told. Walking into the warm kitchen he saw Mama sitting at the table sealing the last of several jars. Papa said, "Carry as many as you can. We will come back for the others."

Jozef picked up six. Inside were Mama and Papa's rings, Mama's locket and Papa's (now his) gold watch. Papa or Mama must have taken it off his bureau. Others held coins and rolled paper money.

Jozef had a very large lump in his throat that he was finding impossible to swallow. He followed Papa out to the garden. Far out by the old apricot trees. The moon was not quite full. If it had not been for the mission they were on, it would have been a pleasant evening.

Once they were standing by the gnarled old apricot tree, fragrant with paper-thin blossoms, they began to dig. Holes, deep holes, Josef could hear his Papa huffing in the night, more so with each new hole.

After they had dug four holes, Jozef asked, "How many more?" Papa said two more should be plenty. Jozef said, "Papa go and get the remaining jars from the kitchen table. I will finish the holes."

Standing with his right foot on the shovel he watched Papa walk to the house. For the first time it struck him that Papa looked like an old man, fragile. An ice-cold stab struck his heart. He jabbed the shovel into the musk sweet earth with a hard and violent thrust.

He quickly had the two holes dug. Papa returned with the three remaining jars and said," That is all Son." Once the jars were in the holes, Jozef covered them, taking care to spread fallen leaves, blossoms, and twigs over the holes. Glancing over their work, no one could tell that underneath these leaves, this earth, were all their earthly belongings.

Jozef suddenly, quietly, began to cry. His father wrapped him in his arms and Jozef felt that his cheeks were damp too. They stood there embracing one another until Jozef finally spoke, "What's going to happen to us Papa?"

His father, never one to speak falsehoods, looked into his son's eyes, and simply said, "I don't know." Arm in arm they walked back to the house.

As fate would have it, very few would reclaim their treasures. The treasures were to be found, years later, when the new owners of their houses planted a garden, repaired a floor or stumbled across them accidentally when remodeling. These treasure—these lost belongings—now belonged to strangers, their history lost forever. They found their way to new places, with new people, all around the world. But along with their beauty, their unique one of a kind craftsmanship some carried a desire not to be forgotten, a constant reminder of a time long gone, a compelling urge to be remembered.

Some might scoff at the idea of an object having a soul. But then, they were not in Poland in 1939, when the world came to an end.

Many years later...

The nightmares came again last night, even more vibrantly real. Gray hued shadows huddled together coming ever closer. Silently at first, moving slowly until they were standing lurking about him some kneeling. With low ever mounting moans that, by the time he woke up drenched in sweat, were once again screaming, terrified, piercing, unending cries.

He had been having these dreams for several months now, but lately more often. Sometimes two or three times a week. Always the same shapes, almost pleading with him to listen, to help. He awoke drenched in sweat with his heart bruising his chest.

The first time it happened he "jumped" awake. Got out of bed and walked briskly into the kitchen. Pouring himself a glass of water he drank it standing by the sink. Slowly, insanely slowly, his heart began to fall back into its regular rhythm. Until he was reasonably sure he was not going to die of a heart attack. He thought briefly of taking an aspirin to be on the safe side.

He stood there letting the images repeat themselves over and over in his mind's eye. Who or what were these dark shadows? What did they want? Where did they come from? He had an overwhelming feeling they wanted something from him. They were a nightmare of the most horrific kind, that was for sure, and yet he didn't feel threatened by them. He felt tremendous sorrow for them.

The nightmares began to haunt his days. Riding the subway home going into a tunnel, he thought he caught a glimpse of one or two of the gray shadows. Silently waiting, almost imploring him, but for what? What reason?

He began to put off his usual bedtime hour, later and later. Many mornings found him asleep in his favorite overstuffed wing back chair. It was those mornings, as he made a cup of coffee, that he would realize that, just as when he was a child, he was afraid to go to sleep afraid of what was to come. Some nights he slept without incident, or thinking about it, not even a good or happy dream, simply a good night's rest. He felt exhausted, so spent; he felt that was the reason the nightmares left him alone.

Tonight, he was having dinner with Rob and Perry, two of his co-workers. They were going to meet at Marbles a trendy new restaurant known for its exotic stiff drinks and haute cuisine. He got there at 7:00 and was early, so he ordered a Cucumbertini and sat at the bar waiting for his friends. The crowd was friendly and the atmosphere pleasingly comfortable.

He had just taken a third sip of his drink, which tasted exactly like a cucumber soaked in vodka, when he glanced in the smoky mirror behind the bar. He dropped his glass shattering it on the counter. There in the mirror he saw three figures, in their usual gray color, standing right behind him.

Mike immediately began to pick up the shattered fragments of his glass, but the bartender beat him to it. Saying, "No problem Sir. I've got this. I'll make you another."

Mike said, "I'm sorry. It just slipped out of my hand." The bartender could tell Mike was rattled but not the edgy "had one too many" kind of rattled. Accidents do happen. He finished wiping up the counter and went to make a fresh cocktail.

Mike was afraid, terrified really, to look in the mirror but look up he did. All he saw was a room filled with tables and people laughing and having a good time. As the bartender returned and set down his fresh drink, Mike said, "Thank you" and immediately felt a hand on his left shoulder.

It was Rob saying, "Oh I see you've started without me."

Mike was so relieved to see a familiar friendly face he slapped Rob on the back saying, "Yeah, I got here a bit early. What'll you have?"

Rob ordered a Guinness saying, "None of those weird drinks for me. Give me a good cold Guinness any day."

They made small talk, mostly about work. Within 15 minutes Perry strolled in, so they took their drinks to the table, Mike leaving a very generous tip behind.

Everyone was in a good mood, nothing more stressful than the weekend ahead of them. They talked about anything but work. Mike said he and Suzanne were planning on a camping trip next weekend. Hard to believe all the supplies you needed just to sleep out under the stars. At that moment Mike caught himself thinking "What if it happens when we're camping in the middle of nowhere?" The thought chilled him. Maybe camping right now wasn't the best thing to do. He knew he could talk Suzanne into a nice hotel, room service, a spa treatment, but there would be questions. He would only be putting the camping trip off. They had been planning it since his birthday.

Suzanne had given him a beautiful antique gold pocket watch for his birthday that was engraved with the name "Woitasgewski" on the back. She said she had found it at a small obscure place down Tilden Avenue. A narrow alleyway really. She said they really should go there together sometime soon just to look around. "It's called Baron's and the old man who runs it seems very kind but not very talkative." She said he just watched her as she marveled over one item, one treasure, after another.

When she finally settled on the gold pocket watch, he almost seemed to hesitate as if reluctant to let it go. Suzanne had taken out her credit card and was looking at him in a questioning way when he shrugged and carefully put the piece into a box. The bell on the door signaled another customer as Suzanne picked up her package and smiling at the gentle old man left. If she had looked back, she would have noticed that he was not smiling.

Mike loved the beautiful old-world charm of the golden pocket watch. He told Suzanne he was honored to own such an amazing piece of art and workmanship. They were both intrigued by the inscription, and surprised that after all these years the watch still kept perfect time.

They opened a bottle of wine and while sipping it Mike kept turning the watch over and over in his hand. There was something about the feel of it. At first cool but then warming almost immediately. If he'd had his eyes closed when Suzanne first gave it to him, he would have guessed it to be made of silk instead of hard metal. It was so sublime to hold. He already felt such joy in owning it. He carried it everywhere safe in his pocket. At night it had a place next to the clock on the nightstand. Truly a once in a lifetime gift.

How odd the way clichés come true, you use them almost daily but never really think of them until they are upon you and you can't refuse them. That's how Mike felt about the one, "My how time flies", and he knew it did. Maybe because he spent so much time awake. Time to think, to sort things out.

Days had literally flown into months. His nightmares continued to the point that before falling asleep he expected them. They still terrified him. He would jump awake time and time again only to realize that once again he was "visited" by the shadows that only seemed to distance themselves from him when he was awake or doing something mundane.

He finally sought out a doctor after Suzanne and a few of his close friends confided in him that he looked like hell and was a mass of raw nerves. He had to agree. He found himself snapping at people.

Once, while waiting for an elevator, a woman had dropped her purse. It made a loud smacking sound on the marble floor. He had jumped at least a foot. The woman apologized as Mike quickly bent to retrieve her purse saying he'd had too much coffee.

The doctor said Mike was overworked and should try to take some time off, get some rest. Mike said that work wouldn't permit that just now, but he would as soon as he could get away. In the meantime, the doctor prescribed some sleeping pills.

For the first few nights, the pills seemed to help. Mike slept through the night without incident. Just when he began to think that the pills were his answer, the nightmares came seeping back, louder, more demanding than before. Mike woke up more exhausted each day than the day before.

He could tell he was slipping. He quarreled with Suzanne about almost anything, little things, like where to go to dinner. One night he snapped at her that if she didn't want to go to Truville's, a steakhouse he wanted to go to, they could just order in pizza.

Suzanne was dressed for the evening and after his outburst she broke into tears. Seeing her standing there, looking like a beautiful little girl who had just received an uncalled-for spanking, he wept for her. Cradling her in his arms he said over and over how sorry he was. He just hadn't been himself and he was so tired, but he had no right to take it out on her.

She told him she was worried about him and had been since his birthday. She said maybe he should talk to a psychiatrist. Not as in "you're losing your mind", but more like a sounding board. To get a feel from a stranger, about what might be causing his nightmares and his lack of sleep.

Mike said he would think about it, but for now wherever she wanted to go to dinner was where they were going. Suzanne hugged him and an hour later they were ordering pizza from Mike's bed.

Mike knew she was right. He also knew she was a treasure. One he didn't want to lose. The next day at work, he made an appointment with a highly recommended psychiatrist. He couldn't really say he was looking forward to it, but he sure as hell was looking for an answer.

Dr. Heldridge was not much older than Mike. He had an easy way about him that made you feel like you were talking to a friend. After a few minutes of questions and some small talk, they got down to the reason for the visit. Dr.

Heldridge asked several questions, but mostly just let Mike talk.

Mike kept repeating that these formless figures, these shadows, seemed to want something from him. He said he didn't feel threatened, he felt pity.

Looking at Dr. Heldridge he said, "I know this sounds crazy, and if it only happened occasionally, I don't think it would be so bothersome. But they are reoccurring to the point I can honestly say the only time I don't see them is when I'm so overly exhausted, I just pass out. When I wake up, I feel like I've been buried for a long time and I'm finally able to take a long deep breath."

Dr. Heldridge sat listening quietly. When Mike's time was up, he offered some sleeping tablets. Saying to give them a try and asking if he would like another appointment. He could make one on his way out. Since he'd already tried sleeping pills, he didn't fill the prescription or make another appointment.

At dinner that night, he and Suzanne were at their favorite place, the Roseville Grille. After ordering, Suzanne asked if he was going to try the pills. Mike said, "No. In all honesty a good night's sleep just isn't worth feeling like you've been hit by several trucks the next day."

As the waiter was placing their plates before them, Suzanne said so suddenly that the waiter jumped, "I've got an idea. Let's go camping. Remember you promised me, and we've yet to go. We have everything we need, and it will be great for you, just what you need. Just the two of us under the stars, so peaceful. It will be perfect and I'm not taking no for an answer. So, don't even try."

Mike, looked at her face filled with concern mingled with hope, and made himself say, "When do we leave?" Suzanne threw her arms around him and they settled on next weekend. With three extra vacation days, it would be a wonderful trip. Strangely Mike was looking forward to the trip.

He thought, "Maybe getting away from the city will be just the ticket."

He was in charge of bringing all the "stuff" while Suzanne was in charge of the food. Telling him, "I know what I can and can't cook on a campfire."

Mike began packing all the gear just as soon as he came home from work. The thought of five days in the country sounded better and better all the time. As he went to pack the clothes he'd need, his eyes fell on the watch on the nightstand. He picked it up but holding it thought it best to leave it home. He didn't want to take a chance of losing it or in some way damaging it. So, he set it back into its place on the nightstand.

He packed everything he needed and added it to the growing heap in his living room. He was just going to check the windows to be sure everything was securely locked when his eyes were drawn to his watch once again. Without hesitation he walked quickly to it. Putting it into a bureau drawer under his socks. Best not to have it on display he thought. Just in case.

He heard the front door being unlocked and knew that Suzanne was here. He hopped over a bundle of clothes on the floor and ran down the hall. Suzanne was laughing and pointing at the rather large mountain of "stuff". Saying, "Will there be room for us in the car too?" Everything fit perfectly. They were finally off on their adventure.

Stopping at a roadside café they had dinner so they wouldn't have to cook that night and could spend their time "setting up camp". The lake they chose was stunning, not very large, with beautiful trees, and lots of hiking paths.

They had been assigned a site and, after getting turned around twice, were finally unpacking and starting to settle in. The spots around them were vacant. They had endless miles to themselves. The site provided a small wooden screened-in building with a large wooden table and connecting benches. In the middle was a fire pit.

Once everything was unpacked and organized, Mike built a fire. Suzanne made a cheese and cracker snack and they had it with a lovely bottle of Cabernet Sauvignon. They huddled together in a blanket on the gigantic log next to the fire. Both were amazed at all the stars. The sky held millions of them. Suzanne said the quiet was deafening. Mike felt completely at ease for the first time in what seemed like years.

Over the next few days they hiked, laughed, washed off in the showers provided just down the dirt road, cooked, and together marveled on the beauty of a nature they had rarely had the chance to see. Mike told Suzanne her cooking was amazing, but Suzanne said an old glove would taste good here. With the fresh air, all the hiking, and the crisp cool nights everything seemed to taste better over an open fire, even the coffee.

Mike slept long dreamless nights. Once even having a dream he remembered about his Nana, happy peaceful dreams. He told Suzanne about it on a hike to the lake the next day, and he added, "You were right. This was just what I needed. I feel more rested than I have felt in a very long time."

Suzanne held his face in her hands and said, "You look more, I don't know, at peace than I have seen you for a while. Must be all this fresh air and home cooking. It suits you. You look like your old self." Mike pulled her tight. They were glad there were no other campers.

The days melted away all too quickly and it was time for them to pack up and head back to the loud chaos that was home. They both hated to leave. They had become so much closer on their trip, with their relationship back on the level as when they first met, fresh and new.

On the long drive home, they held hands but spoke little. Both silently enjoying each other's company and thinking over the magic they were leaving behind. Knowing that they were also taking it along with them.

Mike had only been home three days before the nightmares started again. His first couple of nights had been dreamless but restless. He awoke more exhausted than when he went to bed. On the third night, he jerked awake, soaked, with the shadows closer and more menacing than ever before. He felt suffocated. The next morning, he was completely frustrated thinking, wondering, if he would ever sleep or rest again like he did in the mountains.

He began to question himself again, his thoughts and actions. Should he have said that? Was he taking that comment the wrong way? At times, he felt like he was losing his mind. It was becoming more and more difficult to make rational decisions.

There was a slight misting rain when he walked out of work that night. A quick glance at this watch told him he had two hours before he was to meet Suzanne. He decided to pop into a small mom & pop liquor store to grab a nice bottle of wine, for dinner.

It was Friday and Suzanne would be staying until Sunday. They planned on visiting the zoo on Saturday. Neither of them had been, even though they had lived in the city for years. He thought maybe a few glasses of wine would help him to unwind, and maybe help him get a good night's sleep. Something he hadn't experienced since they had been camping.

He strolled over to the wine selections. For being such a small shop, they seemed to have an enormous selection. He was standing in the middle of the third aisle holding what looked like a very nice bottle of Merlot. Funny how he often made his choice on the appearance of the bottle, the label. Most times he was not disappointed. He was just about to choose the one he held in his hand when he overheard two elderly ladies talking in the next aisle. They were laughing and one of them was saying how nice a glass of red wine was with her homemade spaghetti and meatballs.

Suddenly the other lady changed the mood by saying, "Well my Ralph is finally back to his old self, but it took months even after he got rid of that old trunk. No more nightmares. He says he feels just fine now. I told him you must be careful when you bring old things, other people's belongings, into your home. I told him you're not just bringing in a beautiful old trunk, but you're also bringing in the thoughts, feelings, and parts of lives, of those who once owned it. That trunk was full of yesterdays, some not good. His nightmares vanished the day he put it on the curb for the trash pickup. He slept like a baby that night. No more bad dreams. I told Ralph when he first brought it home from the antique auction, but would he listen to me his mother? No. What does a mother know? No matter how big they get, they still don't listen. I might as well save my breath."

The other lady said, "Pearl, you tried. The important thing is he's over those horrible dreams and now sleeps like a newborn again. I'm going to get a six-pack of that new apple cider. It's delicious. I'll give you a bottle." And with that, they walked to the register.

Mike put the bottle he was holding back on the shelf before he dropped it. He was shaking. Suddenly it was all clear. Like walking out of a fog into a sunny day. The watch... Yes, yes, it all made sense now. The lady was right. Certain objects must carry, hang on to, a part of their past. The watch, his watch, carried just such a curse. It seemed insane that such a beautiful gift could be the reason behind all his sleepless nights, all the nightmares, but it made sense. The first good, dreamless, blissful nights he had had were when he and Suzanne were camping. He had attributed it to the clean fresh air, the hiking, Suzanne, but on those nights the watch had been left safely behind. Waiting for him in his dresser. The nightmares began just days after their return home.

His mind raced for the name of the shop, the street, Baron's on Tilden! He remembered Suzanne telling him they needed to go there together. He walked quickly out of the liquor store and hailed a taxi. Telling the driver, "Baron's on Tilden Avenue."

The driver took him just a couple of blocks away. Thinking he could have walked Mike handed him a $20 and got out. The driver said, "Mister your change."

He said, "Keep it."

He was halfway down Tilden, one of the few old brick lined streets the city hadn't gotten around to repairing yet, when he spotted Baron's. It was a small aging sort of "hole in the wall" place. He was surprised that Suzanne had gone into such a place by herself. When he pushed the door open a bell announced his arrival.

The old man was standing behind a counter in a room filled to overflowing with clocks, some ticking, some not, pictures, family portraits, and vases. Some stuffed animal heads glared at him from the walls. The counters were filled with cases of jewelry, watches, and fragile objects.

For some reason he felt uncomfortable. He walked up to the counter and placed the watch onto the counter. He introduced himself and shook Mr. Baron's hand.

Mike explained that his girlfriend had given him the watch for his birthday, and he was wondering if he could tell him anything about it. Mr. Baron picked the timepiece up from the counter and closely looked at it. He said, "Yes, yes, I remember it and the lovely young lady who purchased it."

Mike said, "Yes, that's Suzanne but I wanted to know about the watch."

Mr. Baron asked, "Is there a problem with it?"

Mike said, "No, it keeps perfect time. I was just wondering if you know where it came from. A bit of history about it?"

Mr. Baron put the watch back on the counter and eyed Mike. Finally saying, "Yes it came in about 18 months ago from a lot I bought from a man who buys out of Poland."

Mike said, "I thought it was Polish by the inscription. I wanted to know more about the watch itself."

Mr. Baron said, "Well the man I buy from, goes to auctions in the district near Warsaw. A lot of the items come from valuables that were found. Dug up when houses were sold, and people wanted to landscape or plant gardens. They dug up treasures of people who had to flee when Hitler took over their land and their towns."

Other than that, he only knew the man as a reputable seller. Who only sold legally obtained merchandise. Items found that people had hoped to reclaim someday.

It was the care in which they had been buried that made them so desirable, so sellable. Treasures once loved lost to them forever. While their owners turned to bones and ash, the treasures remained.

Mike's face was so ashen that Mr. Baron asked if he'd like a glass of water. Looking up from the counter, he said, "Excuse me?" Mr. Baron repeated the question and Mike replied, "No thank you." He simply turned, picked up the watch, and walked out the door. The bell rang in his ears. He knew what he had to do.

He walked the 10 blocks taking care not to put his hand in his pocket, not to touch the watch again. He walked deliberately, as if this had been the reason for the walk all along.
Twenty minutes later he was standing on a bridge over the river. He thought briefly, "How odd, musty, a river smells at night". A light fog was closing in. Making the streetlights look like they were wrapped in cobwebs. He was alone on the bridge.

It was strange how people didn't take evening walks like they used to. His grandparents had always gone for a walk after dinner and the dishes done. But he was relieved to be alone.

Slowly he put his right hand into his pocket and withdrew the watch. The beautiful gift from his girl, the present she had been so proud to give. The one he had been so surprised and pleased to receive. And yet, as much as it physically hurt him, with one deft motion he threw it with all his might, as hard as he could, into the river. He shuddered when he heard the splash. It was gone.

Tonight, at dinner he would tell Suzanne the truth. Then just as quickly as he thought that, he thought again. "No, I'll give it a few nights." If what the lady in the store, Mr. Baron, and the feeling in his own heart told him were right, his nightmares would have vanished with that splash. He knew he was right. Already he felt lighter, as though a burden had been lifted from him. The shadows were gone. He was once again a free man. He knew this for sure.

There was time to tell Suzanne later. She would be as amazed as he was. She would also be relieved that his nightmares were gone. Together they would talk, wonder about, what had caused the taint that clung to the watch. But in all honesty, they would never truly know. Emotions, feelings are felt, impossible to put into words. All that truly mattered was that he was a free man once again. The shroud lifted. The shadows now lurking at the bottom of the river, lost forever.

Three years later...

Helen told Noah he could go into the shallow part of the river, but only up to his waist. She would be coming in herself with Adeline as soon as she put some sunscreen on them both. It was a perfect end of a summer day, still warm but not so ghastly hot. She knew the kids wanted a final picnic before starting back to school.

After sorting things on the blanket and making sure that she and Addie were both lathered up, she put the three-year-old on her hip and headed towards the water.

Just as she was nearing the river, she saw Noah holding something up high in the air and running towards her and the baby with his face beaming. His arm stretched up towards the sky. The glare from the small golden object was blinding...

Deep feelings of confusion
Unknown haze
Matched by a day
Filled with fields of swaying green
In tune to the cries of
Seagulls...

Gullane, Scotland
January 8, 1971

Odontophobia Part I

I have a phobia about dentists; going back to my early twenties. I had been living in Paris for some time. Everyone warned me about the water, so I only drank Coca Cola. Drinking only Coke rotted one of my back teeth. It became very painful.

When I returned to the States my Coke rotted tooth became too much for me to bear. My Mother found a dentist (in the loosest term of the word) in a fly by night neighborhood. We went to his seedy office over a hardware store, at about 10:00 at night. I think maybe he was drunk; or maybe he just had a hangover from the days drinking? He didn't look, or act, like a dentist. More like a backup actor in an old Bogart movie, stupid but full of muscle. His office looked a bit like him, shabby. When he motioned for me to get into the chair, I truly wanted to leave, immediately! Unfortunately, my tooth was hurting like hell. So, into the chair I climbed.

Here's where the horror story, and my still existing phobia, forty-four years later, begins.

The dentist did not wash his hands, put on an apron or gloves, or do anything dentist like. He said, "Open your mouth." As if I were an inconvenience to him and keeping him from his bottle of cheap whisky. He didn't even ask "How did this happen?" or say, "My, my, my, we have an infected little tooth here!" Instead he reached for some tools (that more than likely had not seen soap and water or any form of sterilization for some time) and began to probe my mouth.

I was only twenty, in tremendous pain, and looking to my Mother, who was standing by somewhat shaken up. I was not going to get any back up from her. My Mom, who I loved dearly and who I knew adored me, well...we'll just have to come out and call it as it was, she was an alcoholic, and had only gotten worse since my dad's death, a few years earlier. Being there for moral support was all I could expect. In a way, it was a comfort. God forbid I be alone with this moron.

During the excruciating probing, I closed my eyes and pictured this man being slowly devoured by hyenas. Not justice enough!

I would have liked to have some gas, nitrous oxide, or for that matter, a quick shot of heroin. Thinking the latter might be more feasible for him. But good old laughing boy didn't have gas. Apparently, he didn't believe in Novocain either. He picked up a huge pair of pliers (from a filthy tray) and proceeded to try to jam them in my mouth. It was like trying to wedge the Jaws of Life into a mouse hole. My lips would only stretch so far. But believe it or not, he got them in! Applause from my Mother, she too must also have thought the feat impossible.

He now grasped my disintegrating Coke tooth with the giant pliers and began to pull. Grunting and perspiring, with beads of sweat dripping onto my lilac crushed velvet top, he carried on like a man possessed. The removal of my tooth seemed to be his only goal in life. A final tug of war, with my tooth shattering into many, many pieces. Blood flying across the room, as though it had been shot out of a child's squirt gun, covering the dentist, the walls, and (of course) me.

I caught a glimpse of my Mom and a look of sheer terror was covering her face. She stood there motionless unable to move, let alone come to my aid.

I fully expected the dentist to put his foot on my blood-covered body, beat his chest, and howl in triumph. Instead, he held up all that remained of my tooth. It looked like a bloody spit ball. He was exhausted and slumped into a chair. His head bowed between his knees.

At this point my Mom came over and asked if I was all right. I was drenched in sweat and blood and couldn't speak, even if I'd wanted to. The good doctor had stuffed my mouth with gauze (more than likely from a box he had bought years ago) and it was now almost completely soaked in the blood I hadn't swallowed. I wanted to scream, cry, and kick him. Instead, I looked at my Mother as if to ask, "Do I look all right?"

My Mother settled with the doctor, who seemed to have rallied by then. I managed to stand up, without passing out, and walked down the countless stairs to the car.

Once home I went straight to bed. My Mom must have had a drink or two because I heard the TV go on. I knew that, in her own way, she had been with me through every tug and pull.

My last thought, before I passed out was, "Dentists have the highest suicide rate among professionals. I hope he is aware of this, and maybe, in the not too distant future, he will become a statistic!"

Odontophobia Part II

Recently, I went to have my teeth cleaned. After seeing four dentists, I finally found one who treated me like the mentally challenged four-year-old that I become at the dentist. Dr. C spoke to me in a very slow soothing manner. When he said he was just going to take a quick look at my teeth, I knew he was my new forever dentist.

My old dentist in San Francisco would always have me arrive early so the nurse could bring me a Quaalude, give it time to kick in, and then call me back. Unfortunately, he moved away, and I lost Dr. B as my dentist.

Finding a new dentist took almost thirty-five years, but I do like him. They no longer make Quaaludes. Dr. C gave me gas, just to look at my teeth! After a very brief look inside my mouth, he scheduled me to come back for a cleaning. I agreed only if it involved gas - lots of gas. My insurance doesn't cover gas, but to me money is no object when it comes to someone fiddling around with my teeth.

Which brings me to a very valid, in my opinion, thought. Who wakes up one day and decides, "I want to be a dentist. I want to put my hands (gloved or not) inside people's mouths." To me you must be somewhat unhinged to want to do that daily. I mean, you never know what's been in there! If they're not good brushers or flossers, need I say more? Just thinking about it makes me both nervous and nauseous.

Dr. C showed me his little metal mirror, once. I was so beside myself; he hid it behind his back. The female hygienist was not on board with my total dread of dentists. She had the nerve to pull out her set of cleaning tools, from the Dark Ages, and place them on the tray in full view of where I was being forced to recline in the dentist chair. I was horrified, and about to tell her so, but she stuck a cardboard x-ray implement, about the size of a book of matches, in my mouth. This left me in no position to speak.

She was just about to sneak out of the room to avoid getting too much radiation from the x-ray machine, when the nurse walked in and saw the tray. The nurse's face mirrored the terror I was feeling but was unable to say. She opened a drawer and whipped out a cloth. She quickly covered the tools and said, "We never let her see these. She gets upset even seeing the mirror." I think my face must have been a bit too smug. The hygienist refused to tell me a story as she cleaned my teeth. Even though I asked her, twice.

Dr. C. came in three times and reassured me he was just next-door, if I needed him. On his way out the third time he said, "Let's turn up the gas." At this point the hygienist could have been chopping my fingers off in thin slices, like a carrot. I would have been oblivious. But I thought to myself, "Yes, lets!"

The good news is I don't have to go to the dentist again for four months. I will, of course, get gas. As I left the office, I'm sure everyone was thinking, "What a good brave girl."

Everyone that is except the hygienist, who was thinking (no doubt), "What an idiot!"...

Old men in overcoats
Haze over sea
The come and go feelings
Of sorrow and me...
Venice 1971

The Eye of the Peacock

The day was dark and oppressive. The sky rumbling with black ominous clouds that threatened to spill their contents at any moment. As Matthew sat waiting for the Number 3 bus, he hoped it would appear before the clouds held true to their warning. Running late this morning, he had failed to grab his umbrella, although a quick glance out the window told him he would need it.

Now waiting on the bus, the few sips of orange juice that had served as his breakfast burned in his stomach. The only other person sitting on the bus bench was an elderly gentleman dressed in a dark charcoal gray overcoat. A black fedora was pulled low on his head, hiding his face almost completely. Only a few gray whiskers protruding from his chin resting on his chest showed. Matthew had intended to say good morning, or at least give a nod in the old man's direction when he first sat down, but the man appeared to be asleep. Instead, he sat down and quietly opened his newspaper.

Hoping that the bus would be on time, maybe even a bit early, he looked down the road. There was no sign of an approaching bus. He began reading his paper just as a light mist began to fall. "Great!" He thought to himself. "Can this day get any worse?" Folding the paper before it became soggy, he once again glanced down the street and was pleased to see his bus only two blocks away. He wondered if he should wake the old man.

When the bus was just about half a block away, Matthew stood to make sure the driver knew to stop. As he stood, the old man reached for his hand without saying a word. Matthew thought, "Perhaps he needs a hand up". The old gentleman grasped Matthew's hand firmly, with his fingers on the outside, as he pressed a small piece of white paper into the palm of Matthew's hand. Just as Matthew was about to say, "Excuse me sir, what is this?" the old man jumped up, sprinted off down the street, and disappeared into an alley.

Exactly at that time, the Number 3 bus pulled to a stop spewing fumes. As the doors slapped open, the driver gave

Matthew a "Come on buddy are you getting on or not" look. Matthew quickly climbed the few steps as the doors swung shut behind him. He nodded to the driver, who looked like he was wishing he was doing anything but driving a bus. Dropping his token into the slot, he spied an empty seat in the back. While walking to it, he kept an eye out the window for the sprinter. No one was in sight.

Once seated, the first thing he did, for some strange reason, was to take a quick look around. Almost as if to see if anyone was watching him. Other than a little girl two seats over, who gave him a curious glance as she pushed her finger up into her nose as far as possible, no one seemed to have even noticed him sit down.

He took one last look out the window, as the bus lurched away from the stop. All he saw was the mist turning into rain. Obviously, the old man was long gone. He turned to the paper he held in his hand. It was about the size of a fortune cookie paper folded in half. Perhaps it was a fortune cookie prediction from the old man, but then again no, he really couldn't have been an old man by the way he ran down the street.

Matthew carefully unfolded the small slip of paper. What was written, in very neat yet small cursive, was simply an address, "613 14th Street". Nothing more. "How odd", Matthew thought. Maybe it was a joke of some kind, or maybe the old man had simply mistaken him for someone else and this small slip of paper had been intended for another.

He slipped the now slightly damp piece of paper into his coat pocket and glanced out the window. The sky showed no sign of changing hue. He sat back hard into his seat. Discontentment jabbing him in his back as he wondered when his car would be repaired, and he would no longer need to depend on public transportation.

After many screeching stops and starts, he finally saw his stop coming into view. He stood to join the Orwellian masses queuing up to exit the bus. Stepping away from the bus, he glanced at the sky, briefly thankful that the rain had held off until he could enter his building.

Walking into the busy lobby, he noticed his reflection in one of the mirrored walls and thought that he looked presentable for his presentation. Waiting for the elevator, his finger touched the damp slip in his pocket. For some reason, it made him feel happy, almost giddy. "Odd" he thought, as he pushed the button for the fourth floor.

The elevator held a handful of people. Some he saw daily. He smiled at them as he got on, and then turned to face forward. Upon reaching the fourth floor, he said, "Excuse me" to a woman in front of him and got off the elevator. He walked down the long windowless corridor to Suite number 424. Entering the airless room full of cubicles, he walked towards the back to one of the farthest desks. Setting his briefcase on his desk, he continued to the Men's room.

Once inside, he washed his hands. Again, thinking of the old-young man who had placed the note into his hand. For a brief second, he felt for it in his pocket intending to throw it into the trash. Instead he pulled out his comb and ran it through his now dry hair. He was about to walk out when Artie walked in.

Artie was the office "nice" guy. The go to guy when you needed something completed, or last-minute touches on an unfinished task. Artie smiled and gave Matthew a soft punch on his upper right arm asking, "All set for the presentation?" Matthew smiled back, "As ready as I'm going to be." "Good, good" Artie said. "Be with you in a minute." He disappeared into a stall.

Matthew was back at his desk when Artie walked by with a grin and a "thumbs up". Matthew gave his papers a quick once over, put them into order, and secured them with a paper clip. He was ready when the loudspeaker announced the eight o'clock meeting was about to start. He stood, walked into the conference room, and took a seat at the far end of the table.

He thought the presentation went as well as could be expected. To Matthew it seemed like objections always had to be made to impress the big shots or to let those around the table know that indeed they had been paying attention. For a moment, Matthew felt like walking out. What was he doing anyway? What was he trying to accomplish? Who was he trying to impress?

He felt the room was too warm. The people too close. He simply wanted to be finished, to be outside in the open air. He was relieved when he felt a few pats on his back and realized that the meeting was over and his presentation undoubtedly a success. He smiled. Said "thank you" several times, and a couple "that's right Sir", and then he was once again on the elevator, heading home.

He thought about stopping at Bobby's Bar and having a scotch before heading home. No real reason to rush home. Who was waiting? Not even a cat to welcome him home after a long, too long, tiring day. He'd turned to walk in the direction of Bobby's, when his hand again felt the paper in his pocket. He took it out and, on impulse, hailed a passing cab and told the driver "613 14th Street".

He settled back into the cab and thought, "What in the hell am I doing?" Before he could change his mind and give the driver his home address, they were pulling up to an old Victorian house. Green and white and set back from the street, it had a gray porch, and trees, lots and lots of trees. A gray wooden staircase led up to the porch.

The driver said, "Here you are Mack", which startled Matthew so much, he jumped. Taking out his wallet, he paid the driver and got out. Never once taking his eyes off the house. The cab vanished. He was left standing alone on the sidewalk.

The day was turning from gray to a darker charcoal. For the first time he felt it getting chilly. He pulled his overcoat tighter, still watching the house that almost seemed to be watching him back. Suddenly he felt like an idiot. What was he doing here? What did he expect to accomplish, to discover? He started to walk away toward a busier street, thinking he'd catch another cab home. He'd have that drink and wonder why he had come here in the first place.

A sliver of light cut the darkness of the porch and caught his attention. A woman, maybe in her forty's, stepped out from the house clutching her purse. Pausing for a moment, she looked around as though confused or unsure. Then she ran down the steps. Once on the sidewalk, she turned sharply right and briskly walked away, out of sight. Matthew had the feeling she was escaping. He looked up at the house. He had noticed a sign above the knocker, before the door closed.

The porch was once again engulfed in darkness, Matthew slowly, trying not to make a sound, started up the old wooden stairs. After what felt like an eternity, he reached the porch. It was too dark to see what the sign said. He lit a match from his pocket and held it up to the heavy gray door. A small wooden sign said in neat cursive, "Treasures Wanted".

Matthew was about to turn and leave, when the door opened so quickly and unexpectedly that a slight cry escaped his lips. He was face to face with a man he judged to be at least eighty years old. Thinning gray hair stood out around his face. It was if someone was holding an electrical horseshoe above his head, creating static electricity. He was a bit pudgy (rotund) and dressed in clothes that reminded Matthew of someone from a different era. His corduroy pants were faded and almost slick. His faded blue shirt was clean, but very old. He wore a maroon sweater vest over it. He looked at Matthew and said, in a not unfriendly voice, "May I help you?"

Matthew felt like a fool. What was he supposed to say to this old man, whose porch he just happened to be trespassing on? Totally baffled, he stammered out, "Well this morning a man gave me this slip of paper." He produced it from his pocket and reluctantly let it slip from his hand into the old man's. Giving it to the old man, made Matthew feel uneasy. Almost as though he wanted it back.

The old man asked, "Who gave this to you?" Matthew told him about the "old man" at the bus stop that morning. He felt uneasy, uncomfortable, standing on the dark porch telling a total stranger why he had come. Wondering at the same time, why had he come?

The man introduced himself as Mr. Chambers. He said that he was the owner of the house and ran a small business from it. Matthew took his pale light green hand into his own and introduced himself. Adding that he felt a bit silly being here. Mr. Chambers face broke into what looked like it was trying to be a smile. He asked, "Would you like to come inside?" Matthew said, "Oh no. I won't be bothering you any further", but found himself being led past the threshold. The door shut silently behind him. They were standing in a very small reception hall with transoms above each of the three doors.

Mr. Chambers was opening the farthest door and Matthew could see a faint orange glow coming from the room. Perhaps from a fireplace, it had an almost cozy feel to it. They walked in and Matthew saw several others seated in the room. The color came from two lamps that glowed orange.

Mr. Chambers said, "A few of my clients. Would you care to have a seat?" The group looked up at him with anxious, strained, faces. Matthew guessed them to range in age from early twenties to an elderly lady who looked to be in her eighty's. The room had the air of a waiting room about it. Not unlike a doctor or dentist's office. Only the furniture gave away the fact it was a house, a home.

Matthew was about to say that he'd best be going, when a woman, with very sharp features and wearing a pale lemon colored linen suit, walked in with a clipboard in her hand. Without acknowledging Matthew, she called out "Mr. Rogers!" A man in his early forty's, dressed much as Matthew, stood and slowly left the room with the woman. The door closed behind them.

Mr. Chambers said to Matthew, "If you'll excuse me." Matthew turned to reply, but he was gone. Matthew was left standing alone. The others went back to their books or papers. One lady sat staring at the ceiling.

Matthew felt very odd. He thought he should just turn and leave. Something made him want to stay. Something held him. It felt unnerving to be left alone in a strange room, in a strange house, with a group of strangers. He walked to a leather wing chair, and sat, collapsed almost, into it. No one said a word. The only sound was a clock ticking loudly somewhere.

Matthew looked around the parlor and was surprised to see glass cases filling almost every inch of the room. They were filled to overflowing. It looked like the collection of someone who couldn't make up his mind what to collect. Beautiful cat-eye marbles were held captive in a large glass jar, right next to bones of an animal. Behind them were dried flowers, perhaps a bridal bouquet at one time. A small basket holding seashells set next to a pearl necklace that looped over the shelf. There was a rusty old horseshoe linked to what looked like a dog collar, once red, now peeling, showing a strip of leather under the once bright collar.

Looking away from the cases for just a minute, he noticed several hats. Some men's top hats, and a few ladies' hats with luxurious velvet flowers sewed on them stacked next to one another. Matthew also noticed a stuffed owl, a turtle shell, and a few bowls. One was carved, the others old, but very beautiful and all looked of museum quality.

In one corner under one of the high windows stood a tall urn, maybe three feet high. The entire urn was covered in a very intricate pattern, which must have taken hour upon hour of labor. Its handles were two cobras. The eyes piercing, necks flared out, almost obscene tails twisting and swirling towards the base. Giving them a frightening almost real look.

The urn was filled to over-flowing with peacock feathers of all sizes, beautifully arranged. Matthew leaned in for a closer look and was startled to see the eyes staring at him. Noticing his every movement. He sat there transfixed by their stare. He felt he was being examined and should be lying on a couch somewhere. Pouring out his heart. Only, these eyes did not seem sympathetic. Instead, they were menacing. Urging him to go, to run. He leaned back into his chair. Removing his gaze, and yet, they followed his every movement. He could not escape the relentless, icy cold, staring eyes.

The objects surrounding him seemed to have no end. Each one unique, different from the one it was placed next to. Space seemed to be limited. However, the room did not feel cluttered. It all fit together like a child's jigsaw puzzle.

Matthew was so absorbed in looking at the objects that for a while he forgot where he was. What he was doing. It was like being at a museum. He wanted to take a closer look at the tall wood case across the room and was just about to slide over to it, when the door jerked open, shattering the stillness of the room. A small cup tinkled on a shelf; the owl swayed but did not fall.

The lady in the pale lemon suit said, "Mr. Evers". Matthew found himself standing and walking to her. She grasped his hand. Her grip was as strong as the roots of an oak. The others in the room looked up briefly and then went straight back to what they had been doing. Matthew wanted to question her and ask where they were going. Instead, he allowed her to lead him down a long hallway lined with pictures. Pictures that they passed too quickly for Matthew to take note of in the dim light.

Light was spilling out of a room at the end of the hall. It was into this room that Matthew was ushered. Standing in the doorway he looked back down the hall, but the lady in the pale lemon suit was nowhere to be seen.

Mr. Chambers was saying, "Come in Mr. Evers. Have a seat". Mr. Chambers was seated at a large, old fashioned, oak desk filled with a vast number of things. Rusty jacks, a small stuffed toy poodle, a carved candle, books, and a toy wind-up monkey that held only one cymbal in its broken hands. Mr. Chamber's office was lined with bookcases full of books as well as many other things. Again, Matthew had to catch himself up and turn towards Mr. Chambers. He longed to look at the assortment surrounding him.

Sitting in the chair offered to him, the only other one in the room, it faced Mr. Chambers, he blurted out, "What is this Place?" Then regaining his composure, he said, "If you don't mind my asking."

Mr. Chambers, who was now smoking a cigar, appeared to be looking at him. While at the same time assessing him, deciding. Finally, he said, in a gritty, strained voice, that truly did seem curious, urgent, "Why it's what you could call a trading post. You may have noticed all my favorites, my treasures."

Matthew said, "You mean all these things are your treasures?" "Yes, yes," replied Mr. Chambers. "Well to be perfectly honest they didn't start out as my treasures. They started out as someone else's, and then we traded."

Matthew stammered out, "For what? What did others get for trading all this stuff, this...junk?" Yes, after a second glance, some of it did look to have value, but why give it to Mr. Chambers? Why did Mr. Chambers want all these things? He abruptly stood up and said, "I have to be going. I don't belong here. I have nothing to trade, and I have nothing I want or need from you."

That's when Mr. Chambers said, "That's where you're wrong Mr. Evers. We do have things to trade."

Matthew sat down again and said, "We do? For what?" Mr. Chambers leaned in closer to Matthew and held his gaze with his greasy, darting eyes. "I, Mr. Evers, can give you something you want, but have yet to find." "Oh really", said Matthew, "and what might that be?" "Contentment, peace of mind" said Mr. Chambers. The words almost dripping from his lips.

"I have total peace of mind and am very content with my life Mr. Chambers" Matthew almost cried out. Slight perspiration began to form on his forehead. Mr. Chambers removed the cigar from his mouth and gave Matthew a look that almost frightened him. How did this stranger know what Matthew wanted most, and yet lacked?

Matthew was unnerved, rattled. Checking himself, he thought, "It's a bluff. Expressing himself a little bit louder than necessary, he said, "Everyone wants peace and contentment." He stood up, but the cigar smoke filled the room with a gray-blue haze, and he started to cough. Mr. Chambers offered a glass of water, which Matthew quickly declined. Matthew fell back into his chair. Never once taking his eyes off Mr. Chamber. Mr. Chamber's gaze never left his either. Mr. Chambers was saying, "Perhaps you'd rather have a brandy?" Matthew nodded yes to this offer.

Mr. Chambers stood and walked to a small table, which held an old decanter and two glasses. After pouring the amber colored liquid a few fingers deep into each glass, he returned to his seat and handed one glass to Matthew. Matthew took the glass and, after a glance at Mr. Chambers, threw it back in one long swallow.

A sly smile crossed Mr. Chamber's face, but Matthew's tilted head did not permit him to observe. Finished, he set his glass on the desk and looked at Mr. Chambers, who was just draining his glass. Clasping his fingers together he said to Matthew, "So why are you here?" Matthew put his right hand to his forehead, and said in a somewhat unsure, quivering voice, "I have no idea."

Mr. Chambers offered another drink. Matthew declined saying, "No, I really should be going." Mr. Chambers said, "Do you need to be somewhere? Is someone waiting for you?" The question stabbed Matthew as sharply as a blade. No, no, he had nowhere to be and no one was waiting for him. This realization hit him like a punch to his chest. The same way he'd felt as a child after a fall. He couldn't breathe. His mother would say that he'd just had the wind knocked out of him. Sitting in this chair, in this smoke-filled room, he felt like the wind had been knocked out of him. He struggled for his next breath.

Matthew finally managed to ask Mr. Chambers if they could crack the window open just a bit. Mr. Chambers stood, the old wooden chair creaking, and walked to one of the very tall windows. He raised it just enough to ruffle some papers on his desk and to allow Matthew to take a long deep breath. It helped. He could feel his head clearing, and for an instant, he felt refreshed. Mr. Chambers, with the cigar still in his mouth said, "Better?" Matthew nodded yes.

After what seemed like forever, Matthew said, "What do you want Mr. Chambers?" Mr. Chambers said, "Remember it was you who came to me. What do you want?"

"I want to be content", Matthew fairly cried out. "I want to feel fulfilled. I want meaning in my life; order, balance, contentment."

"Well then, you've come to the right place," said Mr. Chambers with a knowing glint in his eye. Matthew feeling somewhat trapped said, "What do I do?" Mr. Chambers said, "You give me a treasure, something you value. It might be utterly valueless to someone else, but it must have great meaning for you. Something you would miss if you lost it."

"Like what?" Matthew asked. "Look around" said Mr. Chambers. "These objects at one time held great meaning, genuine value, for someone. It was not an easy thing for their owners to part with them. The more sorrow the parting gives you, the greater your contentment will be. I have no desire to trivialize this act of giving up. I understand it is a painful one, but alas, they are only things. In return you will have happiness, peace."

"The greater the sacrifice, the greater the peace" Matthew sighed, sitting back into his chair. He muttered softly, "How?"

Mr. Chambers asked, "What do you have to trade?"

Matthew sat silent for a few moments his eyes shut tightly against the pain he was feeling. Then it became clear to him. Almost like a bolt the thought came to him. "My Eagle Scout pin." He valued the pin above all else of his childhood things. He could still remember the day it was awarded to him. The first time he had felt true joy, true contentment. "A job well done" his scout leader had said as he pinned it onto his sash. In his entire troop he had been one of three to win the highly sought-after prize. Endless hours of hard work and discipline had gone into that memento. He knew, and he was right, that he would remember it always. Giving up this treasured item would indeed be painful. In a sense, it would be giving away a piece,-of himself. A moment, from the past, that could never be recaptured. Memories, as fragile as mist, can become cloudy. Bits missing. A thing, something tangible that you could hold, could last forever. How would he feel if it were gone? Could he let it pass, from the hands that had once earned it, into the fat little piggy hands of Mr. Chambers? To do what? To set on a shelf somewhere in this decaying old house, left to rot with the rest of all these treasures? The thought made him nauseous.

Looking up at Mr. Chambers he said, "And how do you give me contentment, peace of mind?" Mr. Chambers had put his cigar into an ashtray shaped like a bird with an open mouth. The chubby brownish green stub rested in its beak. He said, "Once your treasure leaves your hand and comes into mine, you will feel a sense of well-being that you have not experienced since you were very young. A tender feeling like you felt when your mother would tuck you in at night or wash a scraped knee and seal it with a kiss. You will immediately feel, remember, that emotion. It will remain with you for days."

Silence engulfed the room. Then Matthew stood very slowly and said," I will think it over, Mr. Chambers, and let you know." Mr. Chambers said, "Fine, fine, think it over and come back to me when you have decided."

When Matthew turned to leave, the lady in the pale lemon suit was standing in the doorway. Her clipboard was missing. She said, "This way Mr. Evers." Matthew followed her down the hall, through the parlor (now empty), and then to the front door. She opened the heavy door as easily as if it were made of tissue paper.

Matthew found himself standing on the dark porch. The night air chilled him and the quiet, the aloneness, felt like drowning. He quickly descended the steps and walked hurriedly to the corner. Once there, he signaled for a cab. When a cab pulled over, he got in, gave his home address, and sat back completely spent.

Back at his apartment, the entire day took on a surreal feeling. He poured himself a scotch, sat in his favorite chair, the one facing the window, and looked out into the night. He knew he should get up and make himself something to eat, but the very thought was beyond anything he could imagine. Sipping at his drink, he closed his eyes and once again pictured himself in that house. Speaking with that man. The vagueness of it now seemed more dreamlike than real.

The next thing he was aware of was a bright light shining in his eyes. He put his hand up to shield his eyes and realized it was sunlight flooding the room. Glancing at his watch, he saw that it showed 8:40. It gave him a start and he jumped up thinking, "I'm late for work!" His scotch fell to the floor, long forgotten. He headed to the shower, only to realize that it was Saturday. He didn't work weekends unless needed.

He showered anyway, letting the steam clear his mind. He put on a pair of sweats and headed to the kitchen where he realized that he was very hungry. After he scrambled a few eggs, he opened the fridge and took out the ketchup and butter. He also put some bread into the toaster and made a cup of instant coffee. Although simple, it was delicious. It was so pleasant to be sitting in his kitchen alone. The thoughts of yesterday, fragmented, almost a memory of a once read book.

It wasn't until he had tidied up the kitchen that he went to find his Eagle Scout pin. "What the hell" he thought. I'll just have a look. He kept it in a drawer in his bedroom and he hadn't looked at, held it, in years. It was in a small box, wrapped in a Boy Scout handkerchief.

Once in his hand the beauty of it struck him anew. Such a simple piece and yet so meaningful. Funny how small things like this pin, a wedding ring, a watch could hold so many memories that just touching them was a special experience. He held it tightly and then let it slip back into the box. Closing the drawer. He walked back into the living room. Opening the window, he looked out on the day. It was sunny with a brisk breeze. The curtains swayed. The day waiting for him, he wondered what to do with it. Without plans, he settled on a jog ending at the corner store for a few groceries. He had never really pictured himself like this. Endless days and nights, void, with no fillers, yellow fading into black. His work, once so important, so impressive, was now a burden, a chain tightening every day. It was time for a change, but what? The question seemed to have no answer. A puzzle he wanted solved, but like a child struggling with a puzzle, the pieces just didn't fit.

Shutting the window harder than necessary, he headed out the door letting it slam behind him. He fairly flew down the cement steps and headed towards the little neighborhood park. The day was crisp, and the park already filled with kids playing on the equipment and mothers with strollers. Matthew did two laps around the small lake then headed back to his street and the small grocery store on the corner. There he purchased a few necessary items. Munching on an apple, he walked home.

A feeling of dread, almost not wanting to go inside, filled him with such overwhelming sorrow that he felt on the verge of tears. Shaking off the urge to sit on the steps and wait for the waves of sadness to pass, he put his key into the lock and headed towards the kitchen. One there, he felt too tired, too exhausted to put away the meager items he had just purchased. Instead he went into the living room and opened all three windows. Putting on a CD he liked, he sat down in his favorite chair. Putting his head back, he closed his eyes. They seemed to weigh a ton.

He had no idea how long he stayed in his chair, the CD playing repeatedly, before he felt he could muster the strength to do the many tasks that awaited him. While doing the simple chores, he could not stop thinking about the turns, the twists his life had taken. Was it that long ago he had enjoyed spending time with friends, even going on occasional dates? Life had seemed so normal, maybe too normal. Dates had turned into marriages for a few friends. Some even turning into parents. He wondered where Jenny was. Was she married with children? Yet here he was alone. Moving quickly up a ladder he no longer wished to climb. Was he so far up this ladder that the only way off was a fall? While pushing to climb higher and faster, his goal in sight, life in all her magical surprising beauty was passing him by. "For what?" he said aloud "For what?" he screamed.

The next thing he knew, he was standing in front of the drawer throwing clothes on the floor as he felt around for the box containing the pin. His pin. He grasped it and knew what he had to do. Changing into a pair of jeans and a sweater, he was out the door before he could have any second thoughts.

Walking almost running he ran one street over and hailed a cab. To the driver he said, "613 14th street." Clutching the box in his lap, he silently urged the driver on. The quicker he got back to Mr. Chambers the better. He was beyond eager. The cab pulled up at the old Victorian. Matthew, tossing some money at the driver, fairly lurched out.

The house almost seemed to welcome him back. He took the stairs at a sprint, two at a time, knocking boldly on the door. To his surprise, relief, Mr. Chambers himself answered the door. The smug look on his face was not lost on Matthew, and yet he didn't care. He simply said, "May I come in?" Mr. Chambers, reaching for his arm, said, "Yes, yes, by all means do come in." They passed the parlor on their way down the long hall to the room they had been in only last night. To Matthew, it seemed like it had been much longer than a few brief hours.

Mr. Chambers went to sit behind his desk. He motioned for Matthew to sit in the seat he had occupied only hours earlier. Neither spoke for a few minutes. They sat eyeing one another, until Mr. Chambers asked, "So, what brings you here today?" Matthew, who suddenly felt like a deflating balloon, said in a voice barely audible, "This", as he placed the box on Mr. Chamber's heavy oak desk, then leaned back into his chair spent. Mr. Chambers took the box into his greedy pig-like fingers and opened it slowly. Taking care when unfolding the pin from the Boy Scout handkerchief. He held the pin up, all the while watching Matthew.

Finally, when Matthew was feeling as though he might burst, Mr. Chambers said, "So you've brought me a treasure". Matthew, perspiration beads on his brow, nodded yes. At the same time, he realized that things had changed. He no longer felt downtrodden. The despair, that had clung to him for some time now, replaced with an almost giddy sensation of boyhood exuberance. He felt light, airy, like mist rising from a morning fog. He felt happy, contented, at peace with the world. He felt like, not just a new man, a new person entirely.

He smiled up at Mr. Chambers all-knowing gaze and said, "I feel remarkable." Mr. Chambers smiled his self-assured smile and said, "The greater the sacrifice, the greater the peace. In trading this pin, this part of your childhood, you have given a piece of great value. You have paid a high price. I accept your trade, and in return, I will hold true to my promise. You will have what you long for, but I caution you, it will not last forever. It is up to you to make your own peace, your own contentment. I have merely given you a start, a push if you will."

Matthew felt so elated. He stood up quickly like a jack in the box popping up from the box that had held it captive. He felt free, joyful. He grabbed Mr. Chamber's hand shaking it in an almost violent manner. He wanted to scream, to shout, that the impossible had been done. He was happy. Happy in a way he had forgotten even existed.

After a few minutes, with Matthew still smiling from ear-to-ear, he said, "What do we do now?" Mr. Chambers, who had never once moved from his chair, replied, "You leave here a happy, peaceful, contented man. It is up to you when, or if you need to return." Matthew said, "Thank you Mr. Chambers. I truly mean it. Thank you from the bottom of my heart." He had a sudden pang of guilt for thinking so poorly of this person. The person who had fulfilled his side of the trade so brilliantly and filled him with an inexplicable sense of well-being.

He walked to the front door, now quite familiar with the route. Walking down the stairs, he glanced back. The house still seemed to be watching him, but not as menacing now, more all-knowing. He didn't care. He felt like a balloon finally released from its string. No longer held captive by thoughts of gloom and hopelessness. Instead free. Life's decisions were his to make. He was able, capable, to make his own choices. Choosing to be happy.

Happiness is a tricky thing. At times it can fall into your lap, when you weren't even seeking it. When pursuing, running after it, often only despair awaits. It can stay. Last for many, many, years or only for one brief second. A brief encounter can fill many voids. Can be taken out and fondled in bleak and lonely times. The important thing to remember, the imperative fact to retain, is that these moments, these fleeting glimpses, are not lasting. Happiness is an illusion, a farce. Finding some, missing others. Some who have it are not even aware of the gift they have, a priceless gift often thrown away like a used tea bag. Others, who long for it, would be willing to trade anything for it. Searching in vain, seekers who never find.

Matthew found out all of this, just weeks after he raced down Mr. Chamber's stairs. How quickly joy can turn into nothing. Moments of pleasure revert to stabs of pain. An ache so tormenting, so much stronger, because for a brief span of time he had known something that had eluded him for so long, it existed now only in his memory, his thoughts, his dreams.

The excruciating part, the unbearable thing, was that he had tasted life's pleasure. He had held it in his hands. Hands now empty...

Pop and Izzy

Pop and Izzy, my Grandparents on my Dads side of the family, were about as southern as you can be (both were born in Tennessee). They moved to Texas a short time after they were first married. There they lived in an immaculate little white house, with black shutters and black doors, in a very old section of Dallas. A long grand drive, covered with small pebbles, ran to their front door. The wheels of their old station wagon always sent the small pebbles flying. I loved the loud crunching sound the tires made. I'd spend my summers visiting them. The memories of those long-ago days still warm my heart. It was a gentle time, a slow and quiet time.

Pop and I would slowly swing on the green and white striped glider on the front porch as Izzy busied herself in her tidy kitchen. Preparing fried okra, fried green tomatoes, and freshly cut up cantaloupe. There was always a jar of perfectly cut squares of cantaloupe in a big glass jar in the icebox.

They saved my Dad's highchair and always brought it out for me on my visits. It was a big beautiful old wooden highchair that my skinny little girl body fit into perfectly. In the sun filled little kitchen we'd all sit eating our meals like it was the most natural thing in the world for a 12-year-old girl to be eating from a highchair.

What I remember most of my visits are the smells. Not just my grandmother's cooking but the gigantic fig tree out the back door that engulfed the entire yard in shade. Its musky earthy fragrance filled the back bedroom.

My grandfather, my Pop, always smelled of Lifeboy soap. Their tiny, set off the back, bedroom always smelled of it too.

Pop collected clocks. All the walls in their back bedroom were filled with clocks. Ticking, ticking, ticking. Some chiming every 15 minutes, others on the half hour, while still others only on the hour. There were a couple of German Black Forest cuckoo clocks that called out the time in loud cuckoos, each one different, each one unique.

I loved them all. Sitting on my grandparent's big tall bed it was a strangely peaceful sound. Listening to all the clocks tick away the time. Something that, at age 12, you think of as never ending.

My favorite clock was an unusual one. It was very pale green celluloid in the shape of a small dome. It had a beautiful round face with stark black numbers. But the enchanting thing about this clock was the bottom half. It had an opening that showed a scene of a cottage with tall hollyhocks framing the white picket fence in the background. A little blond girl was swinging on a swing, that ticked off the time.

At night there was a light you could turn on. She looked like she was swinging in the moonlight. I never grew bored looking at her and hearing the sweet tick of the swing. A never tiring little girl on her always swinging swing.

Many years later, I had a baby girl of my own. On Pop's 90th birthday he left this world, but he had arranged for this sweet little girl clock to come to me. It is one of my most treasured belongings.

Spending time with my grandparents was always special. For that brief time, I was an only child. Dotted on by my Dads mom and dad.

They had a close friend, Pearl, who lived down the street. She made cornbread for my grandparents. I never really understood why my grandmother didn't make her own since she was such a wonderful cook. Once a day it was my duty to run down to Pearl's house and bring home the still warm cornbread for what Pop and Izzy called supper. A term never used in Great Neck Long Island.

Pop and Izzy's house was just a few blocks, from Fair Park. A place where the State Fair was held every summer with Big Tex looming over the crowds. Big Tex stands 55 feet tall and is dressed as a cowboy. In a soft-spoken yet loud voice he welcomes everyone to the fair with a southern twang and a "Welcome Y'all".

We never went to the fair. Perhaps it happened after I had already returned to New York or maybe because Pop and Izzy were both very good stewards of their money. Anyway, we never went. But Fair Park had several museums and an aquarium, all of them free at that time. Pop and I went to them once a week. It was usually deserted with us being two of only a handful of people.

I loved all the museums and the way Pop and I walked hand in hand from one museum to the next. Pop sort of puffing up a storm the way he did when he was tired or excited. He could really puff up a storm when he watched wrestling on TV. He was a tall man, like my Dad, well over six feet and of a large structure. He had been a mail carrier all his life, until he retired. He was very proud of this fact. The fact that he had been in the newspaper in Dallas for having a pack of dogs that followed him everywhere on his route, only added to his pride. Back in the days when postmen carried stamps and could make change. Always having the time to stop and chat with those on his route. On a hot summer day, accepting a fresh glass of homemade lemonade from one house after another.

My grandparents belonged to a "Rolling Baptist" church. Something I had never seen or even knew existed living the life I did in New York and attending a private parochial school, St. Aloysius. The Sisters of Mercy in their long black habits had religion right on schedule and would never have stood for a priest telling, yelling for, people to come to the alter and be forgiven.

In the little white clapboard church, with the windows open in the hope of catching a breeze, my grandparents and I would sit and sing. I would watch wide eyed as one after another came streaming down the center aisle saying, "I'm coming Jesus." Crying and carrying on like nothing I had ever seen before.

At St. Aloysius you sat, stood, sang, and kneeled when told to and not a second sooner. This little church, which to me seemed like a free for all was fascinating.

I looked forward to going to church every Sunday. At home Mass was something I always tried to get out of going to. I remember one time; I knew my Mom was upstairs getting dressed. She had called out to me a couple of times telling me to get ready. I had pretended that I didn't hear her. I was watching TV and really didn't want to go. I had enough of St Aloysius five days a week. When my Mom came down, and I wasn't ready, well, there was hell to pay. It was too late to get dressed so she left without me, with a curt remark over her shoulder that we'd have a talk when she got home. I knew I was in trouble, but I didn't care. It was worth not having to go and sit in church. At Pop and Izzy's church you could wear what you wanted to, and no one told you when to sit, stand, or kneel.

About this time, a mall, the first in Dallas, opened. It was not too far from Pop and Izzy's house, it was called "Big Town". It was a new experience. What really made it amazing was it was the first air-conditioned mall in Texas.

After parking Pop's old station wagon on the steaming hot pavement with the Texas sun beating down on us, we opened the doors to Big Town and immediately were slapped in the face with the cold sting of air conditioning. It was a slice of heaven! We walked from shop to shop surrounded by cold air.

Pop was really puffing on the ride home. He had enjoyed it so much, we all had.

When at Pop and Izzy's, I always slept in the bed my dad was born in. A big old four poster bed with an apricot colored satin bedspread that Izzy folded down each evening. Even a sheet was too much on those hot unforgiving nights. Drifting off to sleep with the clocks ticking in the next room, it was comforting to know that in the morning we would all be up early and sitting in the kitchen to enjoy breakfast together.

Pop was a walker. I guess after years of being a mailman he just got in the habit. After we finished putting the kitchen to rights, Pop and I would take hands and strike out for a walk.

He taught me so much on these walks. He'd tell me about trees, flowers, birds, squirrels, and then he'd talk about events happening in the world. I'd walk alongside of him, soaking up all he had to say. Looking at the things he pointed out to me, seeing them in a new and different light.

He never spoke to me the way adults speak to a child. He talked to me as an equal. Something my Dad inherited from him as he always treated me the same.

I always looked forward to walks with Pop. When he'd come to visit us in New York (Long Island) we'd take long walks down to Manhasset Bay, which was just down the hill (Vista Hill) at the end of our street. It was so close I could hear the ship whistles all night long, a sad and lonesome cry. I never got to go close to the bay. My parents forbade me from going, but with Pop we could go wherever we wanted.

Our first trip to the bay showed me it was further away than it sounded. Up close it was scary. Black water with all kinds of boats making their way in and out of the channel. Pop knew the names of a lot of the boats and what their purpose was. With him holding my hand it wasn't quite so scary but still I didn't want to go any closer.

We'd stand for quite some time just soaking up the sun and the sights. The smells of the sun warmed creosote mingling with the smells of the busy harbor. Seeing what I had only heard before was thrilling.

Pop usually needed to meditate for a while once we got home. That's what he called taking a nap. Many a time I would accidentally walk in on him, maybe lying on the couch, and ask him if I had woken him up. He'd say, "No, I was just meditating."

Pop always had time for me. Never thought my questions silly or too numerous. He was always happy, indeed eager, to spend time with me. My parents both worked. I had as little connection with my sister as possible. Being able to count on Pop's faithfulness was a comfort I still carry with me today.

Izzy was an interesting grandmother. Meticulous about her appearance, her house always immaculate. She was a good cook but not a happy one. To her cooking was more of an obligation a duty to be performed.

I often wondered how, why, she and my grandfather came to be one. I once heard my parents talking in the breakfast nook off the kitchen about Pop and Izzy. It left me with the general impression that my Pop had married Izzy because, while they had been sweethearts when he left to join the military in World War I, Izzy had become (as they used to say) in the family way. Upon his return my grandfather had married her. I had often wondered why my Uncle Tommy and my Dad, the only children Pop and Izzy had, did not look like brothers. But it does happen, so I let it go. After hearing the story, well overhearing, I think I loved my Pop even more.

Pop died just one week after our first daughter was born. It was his 90th Birthday...

The Game

The game starts as a solo player. It is only in playing for a while that you pick up fellow players.

One turns into two. The game begins with a new aspect. The dice roll up and down. There are twists and turns, some good some not. Nobody wants to stop the game. No one wants to quit playing. The game goes on.

Now there are three players. The stakes are higher. The ups and downs felt more keenly.

Quickly three turns into four. The game is picking up speed. At times you want to call for a time out, but you hold your place. You stay in the game. But are you really? Or is it merely the game making you believe that you are? You plan moves that crumble before you can even set them in motion.

The final player, number five, has joined the game. You scramble to find your place and you struggle to keep it. The game ebbs. Taking on a different perspective than when if first began, how quickly two players became five. The board is spinning. As quickly as the new players came, they are gone, off to start new games of their own.

The two original players are left. But changed, so very changed, from the first two who started the game. They continue to play, but with little or no enthusiasm. No one wants to be the first to quit. No one wants to say I'm done.

The choice is not theirs to make it belongs to the game. The game decides who quits and when. It's then that you know you lost control the minute you let one become two.

The minute the game began...

Fossil Rim 2015

Lydia
Pain on a Train

Recently, I took a train from the small town of Cleburne Texas to Little Rock Arkansas. I had been looking forward to the trip, a change of scenery and a short jaunt. It's always difficult for me to be away from home for long. I miss my "dogs" and it also requires a bit of planning, securing their pet sitter. Aunt Mary is always booked months in advance. My kids love her and look forward to being in her care, which gives me total peace of mind.

I had just returned from a month in my favorite place on earth, my Scotland, a few months prior. Aunt Mary had spoiled my already overly indulged babies to the point that, when I returned, they looked at me with disdain. I had no problem hopping onto the train in Cleburne. The station was well preserved. It looked exactly as it must have back in the 1930's at the time it was built.

Once aboard, a train employee told me to follow him up a winding metal staircase that reminded me very much of a London double-decker bus. He led me to a very large comfortable seat next to a window.

The day was spectacular. A perfect day for a train ride with millions of cotton balls fading into a clear pale blue sky. I settled in. Put my leg rest up and arranged my "gear" next to me. Ready to read or write when, or if, the scenery began to tire me.

The train had a very gentle lulling motion to it. Although my eighty-six-year-old neighbor had kindly pointed out a very dreadful train crash just days prior. Still, I felt more peaceful than when flying ten to twelve hours overseas. The train ride also lacked the pressure in my ears that always unnerved me on long flights. I feel the need to stay wide-awake (fighting off the sleeping and anti-anxiety pills I have taken) to help the pilot fly the plane. My constant and steady stream of guiding him on, assures all on board of a safe arrival.

The train rocking me past; old cemeteries, hobo camps, houses built frightfully close to the track, open vast spaces, filled me with tranquility. I felt comfortable and relaxed.

Train travel is slow going which is nice. Harkening back to the days when people took their time. Taking their ease on porch swings watching fireflies light up the night, on a warm Spring night. Sipping ice-cold lemonade on a stifling summer day in the South when beads of perspiration never left your forehead. A simple time. My grandparents on my dad's side, Pop and Izzy, lived in Dallas Texas. Big D little A would never fly. Relying on trains to get them where they wanted to go. Time and again we'd meet them at Central Station in Manhattan, with them having just arrived (by train) from Texas.

Our train, the Texas Eagle, stopped to pick up new passengers in Dallas Texas and this is where my solitude was shattered for the duration of the next seven and a half hours. The trainman brought a plague to the seat next to me disguised in the form of a seventy something woman name Lydia. After a brief introduction, I made the enormous mistake of asking her where she was going. She was headed to Chicago to celebrate the one-year anniversary of her husband Bob's death and to check on her daughter who was dying of cancer. From then on, the tranquility of my journey was shattered.

Lydia took me from the moment Bob first felt "funny" right up to his dying breath. No day left undocumented. I took a quick glance out the window, as we were rolling past Louisiana, to catch a lake surrounded by trees and one lone rowboat with a solitary man standing in it fishing pole in hand. Immediately I felt Lydia's hand on mine to, once again, to capture my attention.

We were not at the third doctor's office visit, hearing the results of yet another series of blood tests. On and on and on. I finally told her I was going to the dining car as I hadn't eaten and with my blood sugar I needed to. Lydia (not missing a beat) said, "Wait, I'll join you." I felt defeated. A quick thought running through my mind, "Do they still have openings between cars?"

I ordered a bagel and told Lydia I was going to the observation car to eat. She said, "Oh yes, lets." I paid the bill and headed upstairs, Lydia right on my heels. She thanked me for dinner then said that it wasn't very good. I was about to apologize when I thought how much nicer it would be to throw Lydia from the train.

Lydia is now discussing her daughter's cancer. How it was an immunity problem that seemed to run in her family. There was no hope for her daughter, who had already medically died three times, but the doctors had succeeded in bringing her back. The first thought I had was, that she probably couldn't take another re-run of her dad's death.

We finished our meal and made our way back to our car. Lydia explaining to me how she had vertigo and the pills she took made her feel dizzy. Unfortunately, there are no longer any open spaces between cars. I looked back over my shoulder and told her to hang onto the overhead rail, which she did.

The sky turned a crimson orange before releasing itself and turning to a smoky gray blue and finally black. The conductor announced that they would be turning the lights off. If you wanted to talk or needed light to go to the observation car, which I longed to do. We were now in Bob's hospital room, with him squeezing Lydia's hand if he understood what she was saying.

I had long ago abandoned all hope of the trip I had planned on, waited for. I resigned myself to that fact. I would be getting off the train at the next station, over an hour away.

The two women behind us were trying to sleep. I had noticed them when I first got on at my stop. One about my age, hard looking, paired with a woman in her early thirty's. I had caught a little bit of their conversation. The younger one saying to the older one that she was living with some guy who had just gotten out of Leavenworth. I would have enjoyed eavesdropping on their conversation but with Lydia going non-stop I could only catch a phrase here and there. Once the lights were off, the car took on the quiet air of a nursery, with everyone curling up and settling down for a long night's rest. The train went on to Chicago with many stops.

Having taken my pills, I felt drowsy but was afraid to fall asleep, lest I miss my stop. I worried needlessly as Lydia was now producing paperwork of the exact cancer her daughter had. She had it in her pocket and continued talking in a way to loud voice. I was uncomfortable and thought that she must be disturbing others. She had been annoying me for what seemed like days.

Suddenly the woman behind us, the older hard one, pulled with more force than needed on the back of my seat in order to stand up, leaned over, and said, "You're keeping me awake. If you want to talk, go to the observation car." I would have liked to have said, "Look lady, I'm not saying a word, she is" and pointed at Lydia. Being a sport, I merely said, "Don't panic, we'll stop talking."

Now, you would think this would put an end to the non-stop stream of unwelcome information I had been enduring. That's where you'd be wrong. Lydia continued with her never-ending stories in a whisper. Which, if possible, only proved to make me hate her more. I was about to tell her to shut the (insert bad word here) up, when the conductor announced, to my relief, "Little Rock". Standing and gathering my things more quickly than necessary, I said, "Well, good-bye Lydia. I wish you only good things." I brushed past her and headed down the step with only one goal in mind, to get the hell off the train.

I have since wondered why this woman was put next to me. Why she ever came into my life, brief as it was. I must admit that I've thought of her since. Wondered how things turned out for her daughter. If she ever got all the hospital paperwork from her husband's death that she so desperately wanted.

I also learned a valuable lesson. When traveling alone and someone, anyone, is seated next to me, I will take out my pen and paper. After a cordial "hello", I will say, "Please excuse me. I have work to do" and never look in their direction again...

The Tide

One

Tommy and Sam had always been bad news friends. The kind of ten-year-old boys most parents did not want their kids to hang around. Nothing major, just rude know it all types who were always disrespectful to their teachers, bullies to their classmates, and always a smart-ass answer for everything.

On Saturdays they'd meet in the lot behind the old abandoned apartment and throw stones at the windows. Egging each other on as to who could break more windows the fastest.

This Saturday they saw a streak of black flash by them when the first window shattered. Sam was after it first with Tommy right behind.

It was a beautiful black and white mama cat with white whiskers. She was trying to escape the corner she had trapped herself in.

Tommy went to grab her. She hissed at him, planting a good bite on his right index finger. He was just about to kick her when Sam said, "No wait." Taking off his jacket he threw it over her, wrapping her up in a tight ball. Then turned to Tommy and said, "I swiped some matches from the corner store. Let's set her on fire. That will teach her for biting you."

Roughly they yanked up the terrified, still fighting, cat by the arms of the jacket and carried the struggling ball out to the field. They chose a spot close to the old wooden fence and threw the now quiet ball to the ground.

Sam reached into his pocket for the matches but stopped when Tommy said, "Wait, what about your jacket?"

Sam said, "I'll tell my old lady I lost it, or someone stole it. She got it at St. Vincent's anyway. She can haul her fat ass out and get me another. Besides, this way it can't run away, and it'll burn faster."

The first match he struck went out in the breeze. The second did too. He had just got the third one going when suddenly two large boards, next to where they were standing, moved with such force they were startled.

There with his head pushed under the boards was Slate the neighborhood dog with a killer reputation. Everyone knew to run or take cover when Slate was on the move.

Slate seemed to access the situation and then was on Tommy before Tommy could even think. Slate knocked Tommy to the ground tearing into his face with blinding white teeth. Blood was spurting everywhere as Slate bit again and again. Tommy screamed in pain until he fell limp.

Sam had been startled too terrified to move. He just stood there in total horror knowing he should run but his legs would not move.

The cat took this chance to unwrap herself and ran to the now safety of the old building. Running for her life and the life of her kittens.

It was her quick movement that made Slate look up from his now still prey and slowly, with a low moaning growl, turn his now blood covered muzzle to Sam.

At this sight, Sam found his legs and began to slowly back away all the while saying, "Nice Slate, nice dog,"

At the mention of his name, Slate was on Sam landing one crushing bite after another into Sam's thin legs. Sam was screaming in pain and begging for help. Abruptly, Slate turned and walked away towards the old clapboard house belonging to Mr. McGregor.

It was the house Mr. McGregor had brought his bride home to a lifetime ago when the neighborhood had been filled with friendly people always eager to give a friend a hand.

Everyone had kept their house tidy and filled the yards with flowers, some even with vegetables. Their house had always been one of the best kept.

Now with Mrs. McGregor gone, three years, it had fallen into ruin. There was only so much Mr. McGregor could do alone. Most days he spent looking out the window and trying to stay warm. He had witnessed the entire incident with the boys and the dog from his window.

He had seen the boys around. They often threw trash in his yard and twice knocked his trashcan over leaving a mess for him.

It was one of these times, a few days ago when they kicked the can over, that Mr. McGregor had encountered Slate. Slate had been rooting through the neighbor's trash looking for food. Mr. McGregor stopped picking up his trash when he saw Slate. He wasn't sure if he should try to slowly go back into the house. Since he was so far from the steps, he decided to stand his ground and speak softly to the cur.

To his surprise, Slate responded by whining and slinking low, not in a menacing manner more in a cowering way. Mr. McGregor had slowly walked into the house. Going quickly to the kitchen he took two hamburgers out of the refrigerator and returned as fast as he could to the street.

He was surprised to see the dog sitting on the porch outside the front door, as though waiting. He walked to one of the two rockers and sitting down he called to him. Slate walked over and the two eyed one another for a minute. Then Mr. McGregor gave him bites of the hamburgers, till they were gone. Slate sat next to the rocker and Mr. McGregor reached down and stroked the dog's sparse coarse fur. He thought, "I just may have a new friend."

This day when Slate came to the back steps, Mr. McGregor let him into the house. Saying, "Good boy. We don't need lads like that do we?"

As he cleaned Slate's face with a warm cloth he said, "I think you saved at least one life today, maybe more."

He fixed Slate a bowl of warm mac and cheese and placed it on the floor next to the kitchen table where he was having his lunch. He heard sirens in the distance. He then made sure all the doors and windows were locked and told Slate, "Your safe with me boy."

Mr. McGregor looked out the window in time to see one boy being lifted on a stretcher into a waiting ambulance. Directly overhead, a helicopter was creating a dust storm as it lowered itself to the vacant lot to pick up the other boy. "Care flighted somewhere," Mr. McGregor thought. Hopefully a lesson learned.

Two days later there was a knock on his door.

Mr. McGregor made sure that Slate was safely locked in the basement and turned the TV up loud as he walked pass it on his way to the door.

The officers were very nice refusing Mr. McGregor's invitation to come inside. They said, "No. We merely wanted to ask if you'd seen anything in the vacant lot behind your house on Saturday afternoon?"

Mr. McGregor said, "I'm sorry. I'm a bit hard of hearing. What do you need?"

They again asked the question. Mr. McGregor had heard the first time. He replied, "No. I was home that day, but I must have drifted off in front of the TV. Do that a lot. Ha, ha. Did something happen?"

The officer said that a dog had attacked two boys, serious too, one was still in ICU and the other had lost his nose and part of his right eye.

Mr. McGregor drew in his breath sharply and said, "Oh my!"

The officer handed him his card, asked him to call if he saw a mangy looking gray dog, and to be on the lookout as the dog was dangerous.

Mr. McGregor said that he would and thanked them for letting him know. "Too bad about those kids," he said.

Two weeks later Mr. McGregor's house joined the other abandoned buildings and a gentle old man with his gray-haired friend slowly made their way in their station wagon for sunny warm Florida...

Two

He never really stood a chance. His Mom was an addict and his Dad was in the wind before he was even born. He had fended for himself all his 16 years.

He gave no thought to bettering himself or in trying to succeed at something. He knew it was useless. He was out only for himself. If he had to hurt someone to get what he wanted, well, that was just too bad. They shouldn't have gotten in his way.

His clothes came from taking them away from others. Beating up another kid for his jacket or shoes didn't bother him. If he wanted it, he was going to get it.

Some days his Mom was around. When she was "normal" (had her fix) she'd cook. Even try to talk to him. In her own way trying to explain how it was. In his mind he simply shut her out, too little too late. Besides who cared what some useless addict's take on life was anyway. He'd just nod at her and say, "Yeah, sure, whatever." She'd give up quickly and go out to "work".

One afternoon he had just punched Charlie, the kid at school with Down Syndrome, because Charlie said his Mom told him not to give his lunch money to anyone but the lunch lady. He had asked for it and when Charlie refused, he punched him in the face knocking out two teeth.

Charlie was crying as he ripped the three bucks out of his hand. He turned and walked away headed to the Mom and Pop store on the corner for a soda and some chips.

On the way there he ran into Johnny. Johnny was a friend, if you could say he had any. He said, "Hey come here. I have something to show you

Stepping into the alley, Johnny opened his jacket to reveal a gun. He said, "Wow, cool." Johnny said he was planning on using it to rob the two old jerks who ran the shop.

He said, "How much do you think you could get?"

Johnny said, "Maybe a couple hundred."

He said, "You want a partner?"

Johnny said, "No man. I can handle those two old crones. But maybe a lookout would be a good idea. I've already done enough time."

Johnny placed the gun in his hand and said, "You hold it on them while I take the money. I'll cut you in for half."

He could feel the excitement in every part of him. "When?" he asked.

"Nothing like now," Johnny said. Together they walked to the shop.

He was tingling. The bell hanging over the door announced their arrival as they entered. The old lady was putting some cans on a shelf. The old man said, "Hello boys," and turned to assist his wife.

No one was in the shop. School was still going on. Most of their business came from kids with a few quarters to spend. Looking for a treat after school.

He said, "Hey old man." Looking up the old man saw a gun pointed right at him and said, "I don't want any trouble. What do you need?"

He said, "Give me all the money in the drawer."

Johnny walked towards the old lady who had begun to cry. The old man walked slowly, trembling, to the register and took out the bills handing them directly to him.

Just then the bell rang out again startling him. He started to fire the gun at the old man. Taking a quick step forward to be at closer range his foot slipped on a roll of hard candy mints throwing him off balance. The gun went off hitting the ceiling. The action caused him to fall hitting his head hard on the sharp corner of the counter.

By the time the police and the ambulance arrived, he had bled out...

Three

She had the kind of long blond curls all mothers hope their little girls will have, eyes the color of wet moss, and a sweet and loving nature. Claire was simply a beautiful child, perfection.

Every day after school her mother took her to the park where she would have a snack and play with her friends. They would then head home to do homework and together make dinner for her dad.

For the past three weeks, a slender very nicely dressed man had been sitting on a bench. Sandwiched between a tree and a trashcan, somewhat hidden but with a full view of a beautiful little girl with long curling blond hair.

If anyone had bothered to look closely at him, they would have noticed that he never glanced at the book he held on his lap. His slanted dull black eyes never leaving the girl.

Once when she and her friends were playing ball, the ball landed directly in front of the man's feet. The little girl ran over to get it and smiling she said, "May I have my ball?"

Her voice was enchanting he thought. He wished she'd speak more but she only held out her arms waiting. Slowly, wanting to have as much time as possible, he bent to pick up the ball, his eyes never leaving her. Once it was in his hands, she stepped forward to take it saying, "Thank you."

He drank in all of her and said, "Your welcome darling." She took the ball and ran back to her friends. He noticed how her hair flew in all directions from the breeze, a magnificent statue come to life.

He kept his silent vigil for weeks, even on rainy days. He'd go in the hope she might show up.

About two weeks after the first time he spoke to her, he saw her again, the moment she entered the play area, this time her mother was not with her. She had come with another lady and three little girls.

They sat at the picnic table laughing while they had their snacks. Then the woman motioned that she would be on the bench and they could play. Holding hands, the four of them went up to the slide and took turns. Then they gathered under a tree close to him and the one, his one, went to the tree and held onto its trunk. She began to count as the others quickly scattered. After a quick glance at the woman, he saw she was talking and laughing with two other women and was not watching her at all.

At the count of 50 the little girl turned and said, "Ready or not here I come," and started to run towards the swings. As she was passing him, he said, "I saw where they went. Do you want me to show you?" She looked at him and said, "Oh no thank you that wouldn't be fair."

He said, "Well I'm here darling if you change your mind." He watched her walk away. This time her hair was in two long braids with soft pink ribbons tied on the ends. As beautiful as the braids were, all the colors of yellow coming into one, he missed her long flowing curls. The way the wind tossed each strand back and forth on the breeze like a feather.

He watched as one by one she found each hiding girl, the found girl screaming with surprise. Soon, all too soon, the woman was calling to all of them. They ran quickly to her voice and each began to gather their backpacks and lunch boxes. Together they climbed the stairs leading out of the park. Watching the last of her as they turned by the big tree he thought, "Tomorrow."

The day was sunny, almost too bright he thought, as he made his way to the park hoping his bench would not be occupied. He quickened his pace.

"A cappuccino with a shot of espresso," she told the overly alert barista, who looked to her like maybe he was sampling too much of the coffee he brewed. He had her order ready quickly. She was grateful for the thick cardboard band fitted around the cup. Just holding it close she could feel the coffee was scalding.

As usual she was running behind. Mr. Myers had already mentioned this to her last week. "Being tardy makes us all tardy," he said.

She fumbled her way into her car, throwing her purse on the passenger seat. Putting the cup in the holder. Once settled she was thinking maybe she wouldn't' be late after all. Relaxing just a bit she picked up the cup to take a sip. The cardboard band slipped off and the intense heat in her hand caused her to try to replace it quickly in the holder. Missing it the coffee spilled fully onto her lap burning her thighs. She looked down and, without meaning to, accidentally accelerated on the gas. Running into a slender nicely dressed man, crushing him between her car and a van that stood parked at the curb...

Oh, how foolish could I be
To think that you would
Leave no mark on me

Thoughts of you will always
Dance inside my head
Reminding me of our sweet bed

But I was young and callous
No one could hold me tight
On so many countless nights

So freely I threw away the key
For I was young and beautiful
So many wanted me...

The Stone

She was working as an activity director at a state-run
nursing home. A shabby run-down place in a shabby run-down
part of town filled with shabby run-down people. Yet she liked
it very much. The people were interesting. Most having
nowhere to go, no family to take them in, unwanted. Some no
longer had control of their faculties and lived in a world all
their own.

She remembered the day she was sitting at her desk
and Betty walked in to tell her that she and Ubee had found a
place to rent and would be moving in a few weeks. They spoke
for a while and she remembered thinking, "How nice for them."
This was back when she had just started and didn't know all
the residents yet. When Megan, the head director, came in she
told her Betty and Ubee were moving away having found a
place. Megan explained to her that Betty's husband had died
years ago and Ubee was her imaginary friend. It was then, she
began to understand that not everyone was what they appeared
to be.

It was a small place, only 25 rooms, with a dining area
and a good-sized community room. It was in this room that she
spent most of her time with the residents. They exercised from
their chairs to music every morning. She would count to ten in
French, English, and Spanish. Some seemed to enjoy learning
new words. Others just went through the motions.

Once a week she would go to the Dollar Store in an area
that, in all truth, frightened her. Once inside, it was like any
other Dollar Store in any neighborhood, sometimes festive,
depending on the season. She would buy (with the money
allotted to her by the home) useful and fun things the residents
could use or enjoy. They won these items by playing a game
called "Guess the Price." She began to get a real feel for who
was most confused while playing this game. They would guess
the price of a pair of slipper socks, a package of crackers, a
candy bar, and so on. Things they needed but had no one to
supply them with, or a treat they could have to themselves. She
would hold up an item, such as a roll of mints, and the
residents would guess anywhere from five cents to thirty

dollars. They had cost fifty-five cents, but no one guessed that. So, she would give the prize to the one who came the closest or needed it most.

They were all gentle souls. Long ago forgotten by those who had promised to cherish them. Some abandoned by fate. Most, would have been homeless had it not been for this little nursing home that took them in. Now that she knew them better, their quirks and fancies, she looked forward to seeing them and hearing their stories, real or imagined.

The only drawback, the one act she did not enjoy performing, was the smoke break. There was a small courtyard off the main living room where the residents who could smoke, did. Her job was to pass out their cigarettes to them. They were only allowed one each, per break time. She also had the only lighter and had to light each cigarette. Being a non-smoker, she disliked the entire ordeal. Once the cigarettes were lit, they would settle into some of the patio chairs and chat with her and one another. This part she enjoyed, minus the smoke and the smell.

During one of these breaks, she left the group to enjoy their cigarettes. She walked around the perimeter of the courtyard and looked at the plants. Looking back at the group, had it not been for the high wall enclosing them, they could have been a group of friends visiting one another.

She was looking at a large orange rose in full bloom, when the stone caught her eye. It was a smooth black stone about five inches long and three inches wide. As soon as she picked it up, she loved it. Cool to the touch and surprisingly heavy for its size, it had a comfortable feel to it. She ran her hand back and forth over its marble like surface and thought it was one of the most perfectly lovely stones she had ever seen. She slipped it into her pocket.

When the smoking break was over, she first made sure all the finished cigarettes were accounted for, then took the residents back inside. They were free to do what they wanted until lunchtime. She went to her office. Sitting at her desk, she placed the stone on the desk in front of her and once again admired it. "Funny", she thought, "how such a simple thing can be so beautiful."

It remained on her desk until the little home closed. Budget cuts could no longer keep the little oasis going. The residents were scattered to the wind. Blown away like chaff, no longer needed, no longer wanted. She put the stone on her desk at home. When she looked at it, it reminded her of all the forgotten people. She often wondered what became of them.

November 7, 2016, 23 years later, her oldest daughter, Esme, called to tell her Leonard Cohen had died. It was comforting to hear such tragic news from someone she loved. She had never met Mr. Cohen. But since the first time she heard him sing, when she was 17, she had loved him. He had been with her always, since that first song. His voice echoed in her mind always. Rejoicing with her when she was happy and lifting her up when she was sad.

Often a line from one of his songs or poems would pop into her mind. Like the night she was stranded in Brussels. It was late and she could not find a hotel. She was sitting in the back of a taxi trying to ask the driver, in her not very good French, if he knew of a place. As he was telling her of one, the line, "We met when we were almost young deep in the green lilac park", kept running through her mind. Comforting in an unsettling time.

She had seen him in concert many times. Once taking all three of her daughters, who grew up listening to him, with her on that Cinderella evening. Now at 82 he was gone. The planet felt different to her. They no longer shared it. He would always be a part of her. She would never lose that. But somehow knowing he no longer shared the same space with her made things feel different.

She had hoped that listening to his songs would be a comfort, but it was not. Instead more of a stab, a pain that brought instant tears with her breath coming faster. It was May before she could finally listen to his songs again. Even then, six months later, she sometimes had to turn a song off.

She was in limbo. Missing hearing him, his voice and his words, yet unable to bear the loss.

Everyone deals with pain and sorrow in their own way. To deal with hers, she decided she had to go to Montreal, a pilgrimage. She had to see his home, his past, his grave, for herself. She needed closure, yes, but even more she needed peace. It was all there waiting for her. His home. His Montreal.

The taxi pulled up to his home. She stood looking at it and his park across the street. When she could take it no more, she walked up the stairs and touched the doorknob. Then slowly, ever so slowly, she walked away.

Next, she went to visit his grave. To pay her respects. Someone had left a small painting on a canvas. A lone black bird perched on a wire against a blue sky. There were flowers and other gifts. Left by those who had also come to pay their respects. Small rocks and stones were everywhere.

In the Jewish faith, stones are left on the grave to ask God to keep his hand on the departed. Stones do no die. They endure. In the words of the Kabbalah, "There are men with hearts of stones and stones with the hearts of men." She took her stone out of her purse, the stone she had kept for so long. She knew she would give it to Mr. Cohen. Just as she knew she would not be able to let it go to anyone else. Even here, standing at his grave the stone felt comforting. She looked for the perfect spot to place it not wanting to disturb any of the others already placed there. She saw a spot, the perfect place. The space seemed to be waiting, almost beckoning. She gently caressed its cool smooth weight, one last time. Then, without hesitation, she used her left hand to place it in the waiting spot.

She lingered, not really wanting to leave. She looked around thinking what a quiet peaceful place. She heard singing; a young woman came walking up. She was quietly singing, "So long Marianne, it's time that we began." She looked up. They smiled at one another. Wanting to give this new visitor time alone, she slowly walked away. As she walked out the gates, she was surprised to realize that she was smiling...

Her apricot vagina
Had turned into a peach...

Smokey

Growing up in Great Neck Long Island, I guess you could say that the Creek our road dead-ended into was my second Mother. At times feeling more like my first mother. My Mom worked full time. My Dad, when not away on business, was usually quite late coming home from work in Manhattan.

I'd come home from St. Aloysius's, change out of my uniform (a must), grab a quick snack and then head straight to the Creek.

She was always waiting and welcoming, definitely my most patient teacher. Never needing to make time for me. Instead, waiting to show and teach me all the wonders my nine-year-old mind could hold.

I spent endless hours learning from Her. I began to feel the seasons coming. Knowing that when the leaves began to change colors, brilliant hues of cherry red and tangerine orange, very soon they would be gone. I would gather them to press into books before they were tossed to the wind, some flying far away, others staying behind to fall into piles that would nourish new roots.

Stark, the trees stood in winter. Black against an ice-cold sky, a different kind of beauty, but beauty just the same.

At school, my classmates would talk of Easter and Spring. I would already be aware of its coming arrival. The trees tight little green fists had told me. By the flowing water of the Creek, green spikes were pushing up the dark fragrant soil. Assuring me that soon daffodils, jonquils, bluebells and wild strawberries would blanket my Creek with both beauty as well as fragrance.

Yes, having a Creek to go to every day was a magnificent thing. I always felt welcomed, safe. At night when my parents would call us home for dinner, Smokey (a Dalmatian/Doberman mix) my ever faithful, loyal, four-legged friend and me, it was always with a feeling of sadness that I would turn to Smokey and say, "Come on we need to go home".

I knew the Creek would be there waiting for us tomorrow. It was still hard to leave Her, and Her beautiful sights and sounds. Making me wonder about the secrets She held at night, different sights and sounds.

There is calmness in a flowing creek, along with a feeling that all is right in the world. I was just a young girl with her dog, and her thoughts, alone together, enjoying one another.

Sometimes, other neighborhood kids would come to play with Her. We had all kinds of games we'd play together. Often taking long walks to where She ended at the bottom of Vista Hill.

Towards Her end, She could be a bit frightening, bleak really, with strange branches falling over large stones and gloomy patches of dark barren spots. Looking as though they were hiding long ago secrets.

This brings me to a part of my childhood, which haunts me still to this day. Oh, I'm not saying it has anything to do with the Creek or even the fact that my parents allowed me to roam the Creek alone. Children in the 50's just did that type of thing. No one really thought it strange to see children outside playing on their own.

My parents always knew where I was. Well, almost always. I also knew to run home when I heard them calling. Smokey and I would sometimes pretend we didn't hear them calling so we could stay longer. When they caught on to that, my parents bought a ships bell, that they hung by the front door and rang when they wanted us home. It rang out loud and true. Making it impossible to say we hadn't heard it.

One late autumn day, almost twilight, I was sitting alone on a gigantic boulder nestled close to the Creek. Investigating the moss growing on the boulder, vibrant green with the touch of velvet. I was thinking of heading towards home, all my friends had already gone home. When a man in his early 20's, dressed in a uniform complete with cap came walking towards me. It was unusual to see a grown up at the Creek. I had never seen him before, he was attractive, and smiled at me, asking my name. Looking back at it now I believe he must have been a student at West Point Academy. There were several West Point students living in our area. I had asked my parents about their uniforms.

When he stopped to chat with me, I wasn't afraid, as he seemed very friendly. I attended a private school and I guess the uniform also helped make him seem familiar and non-threatening. When I jumped down from the boulder and started up the small hill going away from the Creek towards home, he followed. Then he sat down on the grass, patting the space next to him in a gesture I took to mean, sit down. I did, but I was also trying to keep an eye out for Smokey.

He asked about my school, grades, all the things most grown-ups usually ask. I told him I lived just a few houses down the road, he said he lived on the other side of the creek. It was nice, pleasant, chatting with him. Just as I was about to say that I'd better go and look for Smokey he said, "What's that?" and pointed at my skirt. It startled me but I said, "My skirt", thinking "What an odd question."

Then he asked, "What's under your skirt?" Having been taught to always respect and answer adults I said, "My slip." I was starting to feel uncomfortable.

I was trying to think of a polite way to say I needed to leave when he leaned in and asked, "What's under your slip?" I said, "My underwear." Feeling helpless now, but still not being sure what to say or do, I was nine. He then asked, "What's under them?"

I remember shrugging my shoulders and feeling trapped, afraid to run, afraid to stay. I said, "I don't know." It was growing darker. We were alone on the grass and a chill was coming on to the evening. I didn't know how to defend myself, how to respond to further questions. I felt totally alone. Did he intend to ask more questions or take action of some sort against me?

I had lived a very protected life up to this point, as far as knowing about, much less dealing with someone who was being inappropriate. He then said, in a commanding voice, "Can I see what's under them?"

I was scared, very scared. I wanted to be home away from him. I said, "No" and quickly stood up hoping he would not pull me down. He didn't move so I said, "I need to find my dog."

Before I could call out for her, Smokey came bounding to me. Smokey did not like anyone near me, especially anyone foreign to her, we were inseparable and had been ever since we adopted her four years earlier from Bite Away Kennels.

Smokey must have sensed my fear. She looked at him in a not too friendly way and began to growl. Her front legs lowering, in a menacing way. I have no doubt Smokey would have attacked him. I was afraid for us both. Pulling on her collar, I took the opportunity to run with her towards home.

I never looked back, Smokey and I ran like the wind.

When I ran in the side door my Mom was in the kitchen making dinner. She asked, "Are you all right? Your cheeks are bright red." Even Smokey was out of breath. I walked over to her and in a quiet voice told her what had just happened.

She turned pale and stopped chopping the vegetables she was preparing. Looking at me she told me to go upstairs and clean up for dinner. She never said a word about the encounter to me. Never asked one question.

Dinner was served as usual with the talk being about my day at school and plans for the upcoming weekend. We never spoke of the incident.

My Mom died when I was just 26. This incident would cause alarm today and, in my opinion, should have then. As far as I know it was never addressed.

No wonder that I love dogs the way that I do. I have always had at least one faithful friend with me, sometimes several. To me a home is not one without a dog.

I often wonder what might have happened if Smokey had not come when she did. Did she know I needed her? I like to think that she did...

WhoWashaLuLu

Sunlight spilled into the room. The smiling fluffy lambs on the wallpaper looked as though they might jump off the walls at any moment to frolic with one another.

The room was clean and orderly with all the little white beds neatly made. The big round pale-yellow table in the middle of the room with its pale pink, blue and mint green chairs eagerly awaiting a puzzle or a picture to be drawn. Sondra with her long blond ringlets seemed oddly out of place at the table. Her head down on her crossed arms and her shoulders occasionally shaking from her sobs.

She was so upset that she didn't hear Martha come into the room and quietly sit down in the mint green chair next to her.

Martha put her thin little arm around Sondra and asked, "Why are you crying?"

Sondra looked up, her enormous blue-grey eyes slightly red, even a tinge swollen. She said, "Because I don't like it here. I don't know anyone, and I miss Emily."

Martha said, "Oh, I know. I understand. I felt the same way too when I first came here. I too was afraid and felt so alone."

"But that was a while ago and now I love it here. Mrs. Hubbard is so nice. She plays with us all the time. The other night she even let us stay up late and catch fireflies until our jars were full."

"She reads to us every night and tucks us in. She always lets us "sneak" an oatmeal raisin cookie when she's baking. We can take turns sitting on her lap. She always hugs us or gives us a kiss on our heads."

"One night, we were all playing and jumping on the bed at bedtime. When she opened the door, we stopped jumping.

We were afraid she'd be upset with us. All she said was, "Be careful my little monkeys."

"At supper time, she always tells the most fun stories. When it's time for one of us to leave again, she always tells them that they will be back. They are just needed for a while somewhere else."

"Once you get to know everyone and Mrs. Hubbard, I know you'll love being here, until it's time for you to leave again. This time, when you leave, you will know that some time you'll be back."

Sondra blinked back the tide of tears that were threatening to spill again. She looked at Martha and said, "Really? You think so?"

Martha said, "I know so. This is my third time back. Now tell me about your last home."

Sondra said slowly, "Well I was best friends with a little girl my same age. Her name was Emily and she had red hair and deep green eyes. She called me "Who WashaLuLu" and we did everything together. We were never apart. Her Mom even set a place for me at the table at every meal. When Emily's brother would get too close to me, Emily would yell, "Mom, Tommy is standing on WhoWashaLuLu's foot." Her Mom would always tell him to move over, or to watch where he was going."

"Tommy would roll his eyes while looking at his Mom. She'd say, "Don't give me that look mister! Everyone had to be very careful around "Breezy" remember? We always had a bowl of water on the kitchen floor for him." Then Tommy would look embarrassed, shrug his shoulders and go outside to play. Emily and I would giggle and run out to play jump rope, or hopscotch."

"Things started to change when Emily met a new friend in kindergarten named Mary Jane. Suddenly, it was Mary Jane this and Mary Jane that. Little by little it was like I just vanished."

"One day after school, Mary Jane came home with Emily to play. Her mom set three plates on the little wooden table in Emily's room. Mary Jane asked, "Is someone else coming?" Emily said to her mom, "It's O.K. Mom. We only need 2 plates of cookies. WhoWashaLuLu went away. I haven't seen her in weeks." Her mom took the plate away and with it my place in Emily's life. She had grown up and had real friends now at school. I was no longer wanted or needed."

Sondra felt the hot tears falling once again. Only this time she didn't have the strength to stop them.

Martha said, "I know. It's happened to me three times now and at first it is hard. But I promise you that in no time you're going to be so happy here."

Sondra looked at Martha hopefully but at the same time a bit doubtful too. She was just about to ask, "When do you know you're leaving again?" when there was the sound of scratching at the door.

Martha jumped up and said, "Sondra meet Breezy." A beautiful longhaired collie with a long narrow muzzle ran up to Sondra and started to lick her face. His tail swished back and forth like a windshield wiper.

Patting him on the head Sondra said, "Do you think we could go and sneak a cookie? I'm starving."

Martha said, "Sure, Mrs. Hubbard is making gingerbread men. Come on."

They raced down the stair into the kitchen with Breezy bringing up the rear.

Mrs. Hubbard heard them coming down the stairs and turned her back, pretending not to see them. They took three cookies, one for Breezy too, and went outside to eat them on the swings.

It was then that Sondra asked, "What do they call this place?"

Martha said, "The Home for Imaginary Friends, of course"…

The Crucifix

My Dad died suddenly when I was seventeen years old. I remember that three nights before he died, we had gone to Baskins and Robbins Ice Cream shop in Northridge California, where we were living at the time. My Dad and I sat in the back at a table eating our ice cream cones. We had so much fun watching a Boy Scout troop drive their Scoutmaster crazy by changing their minds every time he had everything ordered. Finally, the Scoutmaster said, "Boys, tell the man what you want!"

We always had a good time together. I was his favorite. Who would, or could, like my older sister? This was before the days of Prozac and things of that order. She needed something, but that's another story.

My Dad seemed a bit tired to me. That, in and of itself, was not unnerving or unusual as he traveled so much and was home so little. It was exhausting for him I'm sure. A few days before he died, I remember mentioning to him that his eyes looked yellowish. I asked him what could be causing that. He didn't really reply. I didn't think much of it at the time. Thinking maybe it had something to do with him being overly tired. A few nights later, I had a sleepover with a friend, and nothing seemed out of the ordinary. We slept little that night.

The next morning as we were deciding what to have for breakfast, my Mom asked us to be quiet because Dad wasn't feeling well. We were in the kitchen making pancakes, when we heard my Mom calling for an ambulance. She wouldn't let me go in to see my Dad.

I kept thinking, "Why does Dad need an ambulance?" We stood in the hallway waiting to find out. After the ambulance arrived, we watched them try to walk Dad out. When he couldn't, even with an ambulance attendant on each side of him, they carried him on a stretcher down the long hallway in front of my friend and me. I tried to get close enough to kiss him. I noticed that his eyes were closed. For a terrifying moment, I thought he was dead. The look on my Mom's and my friend's faces told me things were not good. I was frightened and felt very alone. I wasn't sure what to say or do. Mom was making phone calls and my friend went home.

Finally, after what seemed like days, my Mom called me in to my Dad's den. She said that my Father was very sick, but she didn't think I should go to the hospital, as he was unresponsive. She wanted me to remember him as he had been. I thought, "What are you saying? Remember him? He will be home soon and feeling fine. Right?"

But on some primeval level, I knew that he wouldn't be coming home. He was gone, lost to us forever. I had a vision of an empty cone lying on a bed with the ice cream melting onto cold hard sheets.

Our extended family arrived and talked to my Mom, but not to me (except my Aunt Bea). I had not been close to her since I was a little girl. I didn't really like her, and I believe the feeling was mutual. I finally asked her what was happening. I thought she would be the one to tell me the truth, since she wouldn't care about my feelings. I was right. She said it was his liver. When I asked for more information, she stood and said, "You only have one liver" and left the room. I sat on my bed stunned. It sounded permanent and not encouraging at all. This was at a time before computers and Google, to research what a liver, or lack of one, does.

I was scared and felt like I was afloat on an inflatable life raft with a tear. It was deflating as my Father was lying in a hospital bed a few miles from me, his life ebbing away. The one person who saw me, who called me "Mon Ami", who believed in me and was never afraid to show it, the one who always told me how beautiful he thought I was. The one who always spoiled me. Even when I was a teenager, he would bring home something every time he went to the store. A long stalk of sugarcane, showing me how to strip away the outer layer and suck the juice out, a gigantic stuffed bear, a new record album, or my favorite candy, always something.

He always had faith in me, which to this day gives me faith in myself. It was because my Dad believed that I could do things that seemed impossible, that I attended UCLA, traveled to New York City when I was eighteen, and found work to support myself there. Because of that faith, I left a wonderful relationship to travel to Europe and the United Kingdom. I will always and forever miss that relationship, but I am happy that I took the leap. I set no bounds on myself because my Dad set none on me. I believed that I could and would succeed at anything I tried, because he always believed that I could and would succeed.

Oh, I failed often, but not without learning something from the failure, becoming a stronger, and better person from the experience. My Dad left me his strength.

My Mom lived ten more years, after the death of my Dad. Existed ten more years would be a more accurate description. She had always been a drinker. With Dad gone, she took to her Vodka and enjoyed drowning in it. Making no attempt to stay afloat. She would stock up on half a gallon at a time. Sometimes it would last for the week. Sometimes, it wouldn't. When she wasn't home, I would dilute it with water. It took her months to discover what I'd been doing. Diluting it allowed us more time to talk and be together.

At eighteen, I was still looking, still hoping, for a parent figure in my life. I never blamed her. She just didn't have the strength to carry on without Dad in her life. He had been her tower. When that tower fell, she had no one else to lean on.

My sister left immediately after we buried my Dad, to live with her new boyfriend. She rarely came home to see us. When she did, she ignored the shape Mom was in and didn't offer any help. I really don't know what kind of help she would have been anyway. It was best not to count on her. Better to try to get along on our own, which we did.

Mom and I missed Dad immensely. We just couldn't come together to talk about him or to share how broken we were without him. We each moved on in our own way, my Mom working and drinking. I, to college where I tried to be a good student.

I didn't have a car, so Raleigh (my bike) and I rode everywhere, to schools, parks, and the beach. Always looking for something or someone, I hoped was just ahead. A hand reached out to me would have been a help, but none was offered. I was treading water. Just enough to stay above the surface but I was getting nowhere. Floating endlessly downstream.

Time moved along without our taking much notice. Mom continued to work. Amazing that she kept it up, coming home to nights of heavy drinking. I did my best to watch over her and always called while traveling. Needing to hear her voice. Our extended family lived in the area but weren't much support for either of us.

After returning from Europe, I came home to be with Mom. I tried to get her interested in gardening and the daily pleasures of life, without a lot of success. I'd watch her as she went to bed each night and observe her ritual. She kept the small golden crucifix that had been on Dad's coffin at her bedside. After finishing her prayers, she would make the sign of the cross with it and lovingly kiss it good night. The crucifix was about three inches wide and four inches tall. Jesus was on the cross. There were holes on three ends where it had been nailed onto Dad's coffin.

The vision of Mom's ritual is as clear today, 45 years later, as when I stood in the dark hallway watching her. I know that in her mind she was not only praying, but also talking to Dad, as her last gesture of the day, kissing him goodnight.

When Mom died, the crucifix came to me. It is my most precious possession. Not only because it is a piece of both my parents. It also holds my Mother's kisses. Kisses my Mom gave lovingly to my Dad, never to me. Kisses I longed for, but never received...

Harmony

Jack woke up to intense pounding in his head. His mouth tasted stale from last nights cigarettes and cheap whisky. Sitting up made his head pound harder. Looking up, he was thankful he had closed the blinds before he fell into bed. Sunlight pouring into his room was the last thing he needed right now. Besides, the Sea Brite Apartment was bad enough under the best of circumstances, let alone facing it with an acute hangover. Sitting up on his bed, he instinctively reached for the pack of cigarettes on the nightstand beside his bed. Lighting one, he lay back down. First punching the pillow to raise his head.

He felt sick. Sick of the cheap room, sick of the persistent smell of cheap liquor, cigarettes, and the constant dankness of the room. Knowing that the ocean was only a few steps away was ironic, almost unbelievable. Sunshine and fresh air was not what came to mind when you thought about the Sea Brite Apartments. Spell it any way you like, bright it was not.

Dark hallways ended in dark stairwells. Dozens of rooms on each floor existed in a honeycomb of filth. Rooms for the lost, the lonely, and the forgotten. The kind of lost that no one ever came looking for.

Jack crushed his cigarette into an already overflowing ashtray and decided that he just might be hungry. Well maybe not hungry, but able to eat. Getting up he grabbed a shirt that was half draped on a chair and half on the floor. He slowly buttoned it up. His head long past throbbing, he quickly thought, "Why can't you take your head off the way you take your shirt off." Grabbing his cigarettes, he was out the door.

Opening the door to the hallway was a quick punch in the face. He pushed on and headed to the stairs. Two flights down the sun was another punch. This time aimed directly to his eyes. He put on his sunglasses and headed to the pier. Once there he could smell the fresh sea air. The gulls circling over his head, were screaming like sirens. He needed coffee and something to settle the bile that was churning in his throat.

He walked into Sinbad's. A small cafe tucked into a tight spot next to the merry-go-round. He sat down at the counter and nodded yes when the waitress appeared with the coffee pot. He took it black. It was strong and snarled back at him as he took his first gulp. It hit his empty stomach like a pebble thrown into a pond. Painfully satisfying. He ordered a couple of eggs, bacon, and some toast.

He rubbed his eyes. They felt like someone had tossed hot sand into them. Taking another gulp of his coffee and setting it back on the counter, he noticed a newspaper by his elbow. He mindlessly picked it up. Glancing at it, while waiting for his food

His suspicions confirmed. Life was going to hell in a handbasket. No different from his own. "A depressed man reading a depressing newspaper," he thought.

Yes, Eloise had left him, and in all truth, with good reason. But maybe a year was too long to be getting over it. If getting over it was even possible. Yes, he had told her time and again he'd change, but he didn't. Nothing changed except the final change. He came home late one night from The Last Call to find her note on the kitchen table. Saying not to try to find her. She wouldn't be found.

He ended up leaving their small bungalow and moving into the Sea Brite. An old apartment complex right on the beach with a reputation for those that didn't fit in with the rest of the world, some of them (if not most) by choice

The newspaper was depressing. What wasn't? The long endless days he spent sleeping one off. Waiting to put a new one on.

Pointless, everything pointless.

He'd once had a real shot at a good life. He and his Eloise had their little house overlooking the canyon, with maybe marriage and kids someday. But all of that had changed when he failed the Bar Exam for the third time.

For Christ sake, what an idiot he'd been. What a fool! He and Eloise had felt sure that he would pass it the first time. Eloise had even planned a little celebration with just a few friends over for drinks. He remembered walking in the door to their hopeful happy faces, only to shake his head no.

It had been downhill from then on. Of course, he expected to pass the second go around. A lot of people needed two attempts. But he was prepared almost knowing the third would be another failure. Hell, at that point he not only expected it, he was almost counting on it. What an excuse to continue his drinking and his nonstop quarreling with Eloise. The whisky made the hurt look on her face blurred.

The waitress put his food in front of him and refilled his mug without asking. His stomach lurched at the sight of the food. But Jack reached for the salt and pepper and started in. He knew he'd feel better. Even if he wasn't sure, he could even keep it down. "Enough," he thought, and started to turn towards the back of the paper to the funnies. Better while he ate, he thought. As he was thumbing through the pages, his eyes caught a small ad in the lower right-hand corner of a page. In not to bold letters the ad read:

Has your life lost its spark? Does it no longer shine? Are you wondering if you want to go on? Then come to a meeting. You will be among friends. We do understand. Let us prove to you that we do. Come to Harmony, 256 Post Street, Suite #3, 7:00 Monday, Wednesday, and Friday nights.

In small letters, almost too small to read, was the sentence:

What do you have to lose?

Jack thought, "What an odd article, and yet how timely." His life had lost both its spark and its shine. If it ever had it to begin with. Thinking quickly of Eloise, he knew it had. Once, long ago.

He finished eating his breakfast. While paying his bill, and leaving a tip, his eyes fell on the newspaper again. Without giving it any thought, he picked it up and put it under his arm.

He strolled out of the restaurant and was headed back to his apartment, when he changed his mind and sat down on a nearby bench overlooking the ocean.

The sun felt good. For a couple of seconds, he almost felt alive again. He sat watching the people walking by and the kids going around on the merry-go-round. The old calliope played an out of time version of The Band Played On.

He wasn't sure how long he sat there but before he knew it the sun was melting into the sea. He stood up and headed for home, if you could call it that.

It only took him ten minutes before he was back at the Sea Brite, climbing the stairs to his floor. Some guy leaning against the wall asked if he had any change. He pushed on. Not even looking back. The room not only looked disheveled. It smelled disheveled.

How did he get to this point? When other men walked into their homes at night, they were greeted with a "Hello Honey" by someone who made the place a home. A place that was clean, with inviting smells coming from the kitchen. He missed all that. At 48, why bother looking to start anew. No one wanted a broken-down older guy who had nothing to show for having lived 48 years, except a tolerance to liquor. No, he was a loser in the truest sense of the word. He had nothing. The knowing of that made him step into a quick shower, find a shirt that was cleaner than the rest, and head out to The Last Call. There he would be greeted by friendly non-judgmental faces who welcomed him to a bar stool for a night of drink.

As he was looking for his watch, his eyes fell on the newspaper, the one from the restaurant. Just for heck of it, he glanced at the ad again. That crazy ad that said what? Looking at it again, he thought for a moment and realized it was Wednesday. There was a meeting tonight. If he hurried, he'd be able to sit in. Not that he really wanted to go. It was more out of curiosity. More not wanting to go to The Last Call. The same night playing over and over. Maybe a change would be good. He took the paper and headed out to look for 256 Post Street #3.

It turned out to be only five or six blocks away. A garage looking structure down a tree lined alley. He walked down the alley feeling like a fool. Yet, it was something different from walking into The Last Call night after night.

Walking down the alley trying not to trip left him breathless. His heart bulging into his throat, he leaned against the side of the entrance to get his bearings. Just then a woman, maybe in her late 30's, walked up and asked if he was looking for Harmony. He nodded his head yes and allowed her to take his arm to Room 3.

Entering the room, he asked her, "Hey what kind of place is this?"

She merely said, "Oh you'll see. My name's Claire, I'm a guide. Come in and have a seat. No one's going to bite you."

The room was quite crowded. He hadn't expected that. He spotted a seat towards the back near a window, but more importantly, by an exit. If this tuned out to be some sort of AA type of nonsense, he wanted to be able to make a hasty retreat.

Sitting down, he looked around and was surprised that the people sitting around him all seemed ordinary. People ranged in age from late 20's to mid-70's. Some dressed in casual attire, while others looked more like him, shabby. A few looked well to do. The only thing they seemed to have in common was a sad almost vacant stare, lost, hopeless. Suddenly a deep feeling of dread came over him. He was one of them. If the room had been lined with mirrors, the mirrors would reflect the same vacant look, finished.

Jack sat upright. A man, perhaps in his middle 60's, walked up to the podium in front of the room. He said simply, "Hello, welcome back to all who know me and welcome to any new visitors. Would any new visitors like to raise their hands?"

Jack wasn't sure if he wanted to raise his hand, but it seemed to have a mind of its own and was already in the air. Two other hands shot up. The speaker continued, "Fine, fine, welcome one and all".

He then gave the most unusual speech Jack had ever heard. It was so incredible that, at first, he thought this must be a joke. Was this assortment of people here for the reason this man was saying? Listening to others speak about not just killing themselves but giving the rest of their lives to someone else. Someone more deserving, desperately wanting to live and enjoy all the wonder of everything, from a bird singing to a Mozart concert. The speaker, who called himself Simon, was in no way suggesting that they rejoin humanity. Give life another chance, so to speak. No, he was telling them that if they had reached the point of no return, rather than just throw their life away, they could, with his help, give it to someone else. A gift only they could give, a once in a lifetime gift. A gift that would make up for all the failed attempts, all the sadness, the grief, and the feeling of hopelessness that greeted them every morning and tucked them in every night.

In other words, they could just let go, but not before doing one last act of kindness, one good and final deed. They could give something they no longer wanted or cherished to someone who wanted or needed it desperately. Why not leave a small piece of yourself behind? After all, you wouldn't need it any longer.

Jack thought, "Someone like an organ donor." Realizing that he was getting caught up in Simon's speech, he took a quick look around the room. He saw that many were sobbing, some quite loudly and unashamedly. Others just looked down into hands folded in their laps. While still others merely nodded heads up and down in agreement.

Jack sat there stunned. He had to admit that, after Eloise left, he had thought about driving his car (back when he owned one) into a tree. Not wanting to hurt anyone else but wanting to put an end to his constant pain and the uselessness of his life. He had thought about it more than once. One particularly difficult night, after a long day of drinking, he had gotten into the car with the intention of it being a one-way ride.

He had driven towards the canyon where it was dark and quiet. He was heading down a hill when he started increasing the weight on the gas pedal. Slowly at first, then more and more pressure. A quick look at the speedometer told him he was up to 65 mph. He continued the pressure, flying past hills and trees. Scanning the trees as they flew by for the one that would do the job. Looking at the gauge it now said 73 mph.

He had just flown by a large gnarled tree that looked perfect. Thinking he'd turn around and give it a go, what the heck. Out of nowhere a flash of red stung his eyes. It was quickly followed by a high piercing scream. He was being pulled over. Staring down, he popped a mint in his mouth. He always kept them on the seat next to him.

He pulled over to the right and prepared himself for the worst. He ran his fingers through his hair and pulled his driver's license from his pocket. Rolling down the window he handed the officer his card while saying, "Good evening sir." The officer took his card. Not responding to the greeting. He told him to stay in the vehicle as he went to run his card and plates. Jack watched him from the rear-view mirror.

After what seemed like an eternity, the officer slowly walked back to Jack's car. He said, "Where's the fire?" Jack said, "Sorry officer. I was listening to the music and guess I just got carried away." The officer looked him over for a while and then said, "Yeah, I know. I've done it before myself." Jack was stunned. He had been wondering whom he could call to bail him out and had pictured himself in hand cuffs. Now this officer was being understanding, even though he had been going so many miles over the speed limit!

As he was handing the license back to Jack, the officer said, "I'm going to let you go this time with just a warning. But drive slowly home." Jack took the license thanking him profusely. He was about to drive away when the officer said, "Oh Sir, one more thing. Turn the radio off." Jack flipped the radio into silence. Made a U turn and headed home, slowly. Especially since the police car was following him out of the canyon. He almost felt like giving his horn a quick beep followed by a friendly wave as the patrol car turned down a different street.

Once home he felt like he had been given a new start, a chance to improve his life. And he had for almost four days. Until, walking down the street one afternoon headed towards home, he had noticed The Last Call and dropped in for one quick drink.

No, his life had turned to ashes. If he had a glimmer of hope, something to want to go on, maybe he would, but he didn't. His days and nights flowed one into another. Unchanged except for the degree of his hangover. He was wasting what had once been a precious gift and he knew it. He knew it was time for this wasted life to come to an end.

As these memories flooded his mind, he was so absorbed in them he was startled when he heard a female voice saying, "Hello I'm Roberta. This may be the last time you will see me. So, I want to tell you my story. I'm 34 years old and until three years ago I was happily married to the most wonderful man on Earth. Together we had a beautiful little girl Mia. She was perfection, my world. To me my life was perfect, full. Everyday a wonderful new adventure filled with love, dreams, and hope for the future. Complete in every way. I was at home one night making dinner, when my neighbor knocked at my door. I froze the moment I saw her face. How is it that even without being told you just know? You know your life is over. My husband Artie and Mia had been killed in a car crash, just a few blocks from home. They had gone to pick up ice cream for dessert."

At this point, Roberta was crying and shaking. Remembering that night, the night that changed her life forever. She went on to say that she tried, really tried to go on. Tried to be strong, to be involved with life again. But no matter how hard she tried, how many meetings she went to, how many other mourning parents she spoke with, she was numb. Each day was more painful than the last, the holidays excruciating.

Even when she forced herself to go to the market, seeing a blonde-haired little girl would unsettle her. To the point she would walk away from her cart. Weeping she'd limp to her car.

Despair had become her home. She no longer wanted to look for happiness. It was a lost key to a room she would never leave.
Until she found the ad in the paper and had found Harmony, here she was understood. Here everyone understood that life is a gift, a gift that is given to you, to do with as you please. How many times had she heard people say, "It's your life"? If it's yours to do with as you please, you could be a janitor or a surgeon. The choice is yours, your life and your choice.

After coming to several meetings, she had realized that sometimes, some things just couldn't be fixed. Can't be made right. Nothing would bring Artie or Mia back and without them she knew beyond any doubt that her life was not worth living. No, all hope was gone. She felt so alone, until Harmony. They had introduced her to Sarah.

Sarah was seven. Close to the same age Mia would have been, if she were alive. Sarah had long blonde hair with gray eyes. Eyes that would be so beautiful, if only they held the sparkle of life, but they were sad. They looked like the eyes of an old woman. They were eyes that knew too much of pain and too little of laughter and fun. Sarah had a very rare form of cancer. A cure would not come in time. Her days were few. There would be no future. The pain filled days of now were all she had.

Roberta had been nervous, almost shy, to walk into Sarah's room that first day. It was dark. Filled with shadows and the sound of hissing machines. Then it stabbed her that if she was frightened how terrified must this little girl be? The small child who knew this room as home, no pretty pink walls, no dolls, stuffed animals, and sunlight spilling onto the floor.

She had stepped into the room forcing a smile that she didn't truly feel. Sarah turned her head and gave Roberta a slight smile. Roberta stepped over to her bed and introduced herself. Telling Sarah, she had come to visit her and maybe even help her. Sarah looked doubtful but held her smile. Roberta sat down and began to talk to her. The way she would have talked to her Mia, soft, warm, and soothing. The kind of warmth that only a mother can give. She felt the strangeness of the situation slipping away. It was just the two of them, alone in a place of peace all their own.

Roberta went back every day to sit and talk, read, and soothe Sarah and (in a way) herself. Sarah was so changed as the days flew by. She had even begun to laugh. Oh, it was a tiny laugh, but a laugh just the same. Sarah's parents were so grateful, so thankful, that Roberta had taken an interest in their child. They cried when Roberta told them of her Mia. They assumed that Harmony was a part of the hospital that sent people to cheer up those who were terminally ill. They never pressed the matter.

Roberta thought how easy it was to entwine yourself into someone's life. Maybe that's the way life worked when only good motives are on your side. Her motives were pure. Perhaps a bit selfish but she was finally beginning to feel a bit of peace and comfort. Knowing that some good would come from her pain, her loss.

Life would go on for Sarah in a happy fulfilling way with days that would be full of wonder, dreams, and love of life instead of days of waking to unbearable pain. Roberta would no longer be forced onward to a destiny she had no desire to meet. Sarah would have a happy wonderful life just as her Mia would, should, have had. A childhood the way a childhood should be. Fun, carefree, full of love, and adventure, not the life she was now leading. Hooked to machines with pitying looks from both strangers and staff.

No instead she would run free. Chasing butterflies. Jumping into piles of autumn leaves. Staring in amazement at a Christmas tree, her Christmas tree. She would enter a magical land that had been lost to her so long ago.

The more time Roberta spent with her Sarah the more determined she became to give her this gift, her once in a lifetime gift.

Turning to thank Simon she smiled and then said to the crowded room, "I will be leaving tomorrow, hopefully to join my Artie and Mia. And Sarah, sweet Sarah, will begin her new life tomorrow. For those of you wondering, maybe even a few still judging, still questioning, I want you to know without the slightest doubt that this is right for me. This is what I should be doing. My destiny if you will. I will be gone, true, but to a better place. A place where they are waiting for me. I will leave behind a legacy in a little girl named Sarah."

At this point, the room exploded. Some people were crying, some cheering, and others were too moved to speak. Several were standing and applauding.

Jack sat in his seat dumbfounded. He felt himself spilling on to the floor like a bag of sugar with a hole in it. He was coming apart. Yet, at the very same time coming together more than he had ever felt. He was as alone as if he were on an island. The sound of the room had died away and he sat alone. Contemplating what he wanted to do.

Once the meeting was over and people had started to dwindle down, he noticed Roberta and Simon hugging near the platform. He waited for Roberta to leave. She smiled at him as she walked out the door. He smiled back and even waved. He then slowly, as though he were treading through waist deep water, walked up to Simon. Looking into his dark gray eyes he simply said, "Hello, my name is Jack. I'm ready to leave."

Simon took his hand and guided him to a chair. Simon with the look of someone who had seen too much, felt too much, grieved too long. Simon said, "Why are you wanting to leave Jack?"

Jack heard himself spilling out his story with Simon still holding on to his hand. Usually this would have made Jack uncomfortable, this intimate gesture with a stranger, but it comforted Jack. Made him feel more and more like sharing his story. He could not believe how defeated he sounded, how broken. Simon nodded with that gaze that seemed to pull Jack towards him but also towards feelings he hadn't expressed or even thought for so long now. Finally, Jack sat back in his chair completely spent.

The night was calm. The neon light falling in the window was welcoming. It was at that moment Jack thought, "I really am just a speck, an unseen grain. My being here or being gone matters only to me. Maybe someone can get some use out of this worn out vehicle. I no longer need it or want it.

He had his eyes closed until Simon softly said, "Jack, you can glue a broken glass back together, but will it hold water?"

Jack looked at him like he had materialized out of nowhere and said slowly, very slowly, "My glass will always leak." He then broke into tears and fell into Simon's arms.

Simon rocked him back and forth saying, "I understand Jack. I understand."

Joseph looked up and was happy to see Jack standing in the doorway. Joseph had begun to look forward to Jack's daily visits. Jack, always managed to sneak in a malt, a comic book, or something to make his hospital stay less boring. It gave him hope. Hope that he would not always be lying in a hospital room tied to the endless freeway of tubes that stuck in his arms and a machine behind him that never stopped beeping.

"Hey Joe, how's it going today?" Jack was saying as he walked into the room and slumped down into the worn plastic chair.

Joseph said, "Okay, about the same." Looking at Joseph you would never know he was sick. He looked like a kid who should be out playing ball or skateboarding or something. It, amazed Jack daily to walk in and see him. Knowing he was dying. The part that really got him was the knowledge that Joseph knew it too. It was just like being stuck in the groove of an old record, repeating, repeating. Jack wanted, needed, to move the needle forward.

He had met Joseph about three weeks after his first visit to Harmony. Sheldon, who had been his guide, had introduced them. They had hit it off on their first meeting. Joseph needed an outside friend. Someone, other than his family, who was willing to spend time with him. When you came right down to it, time was not something Joseph had.

Jack looked a bit rough around the edges. But he had a quick smile, knew endless funny jokes, and seemed very interested in making Joseph feel more relaxed and comfortable. They were an odd couple. A 12-year-old boy confined to a hospital bed, one he would not be walking away from, and Jack, who sometimes reeked of booze and always looked like he could use some looking after himself. Once, when Jack was visiting during lunchtime, the nurse brought a tray in for Jack. They ate together. While it wasn't the best, it was as Jack said, "passable".

They talked about life. Joseph's life since he was first diagnosed. Jack told him about his life, mostly about how he loved to "knock around" the beach when he was Joseph's age. The way he hitched a ride on the back of the trolley car. Sometimes the driver would see him and kick him and his buddies off. Other times the driver knew but said nothing.

He told him about how good a corn dog tasted when mixed with sea air. About how he and his best friend Tommy once tried smoking a cigarette Tommy had taken from his Mom's purse. What big shots they had felt like lighting it up, then passing it back and forth. Some of the other neighborhood kids had seen them and looked at them in awe. Yeah, awe all right, right up until Jack noticed Tommy was looking sort of green and he felt the same way. Oh well, a lesson learned for them.

Jack told him how he and Tommy had remained best friends in High School. Sharing long talks about their first loves, first broken hearts, first everything. They had even gone into the Military together, knowing they always had each other's back.

Jack even broke his long ago promise to himself, of never talking about the day Tommy died, right in front of him. Jack was just about to run after Tommy, yelling to him to take cover/shelter behind some boulders when Tommy, who had just looked back at Jack, was gone. He caught a quick glimpse of a leg flying skyward before he even realized what had happened. Jack didn't go into all the exact details with Joseph (a land mine on a lone deserted road in the middle of some god-forsaken desert in the middle of nowhere), but he did tell him, that Tommy had died. About how alone and abandoned he had and at times still felt.

Joseph had reached out his hand to Jack. It was then Jack noticed that two wet lines were running towards Joseph's mouth. Jack quickly changed the subject saying, "Look Joseph, I don't want to cause you any more pain than you already have buddy. I just want to be real with you and that means sharing the good with the bad."

Jack said, "How about if I run down the street and get us both a sundae?"

Joseph smiled and bravely said, "Great, I'd like hot fudge."

Jack said, "Two hot fudge sundaes coming right up. I'll be back in a jiff." He was, the bag hidden under his jacket.

Joseph told him Cruella (their name for his nurse) had just left so they had time. They sat eating their sundaes and talking about happier times for Jack.

That night as he was leaving, he said to Joseph, "I'll be back tomorrow with a surprise that will be a million times better than a hot fudge sundae.

Joseph smiled and said, "Just bring yourself, present enough for me."

Jack showered and put on his best outfit. Today was the day. He had stood before everyone at Harmony last night and, like Roberta, told them they wouldn't be seeing him again. He had told everyone all about Joseph. How happy, anxious really, he was to give his gift. No finer boy could be found anywhere. His only regret was that he wouldn't be around to see him grow into the man he would become. But without his gift, that wasn't going to happen anyway. Besides, somehow, he knew he'd know.

It had been a wonderful warm reassuring night. So, this morning he took his time to dress nice. On the way to the hospital he really looked at the blueness of the sky, the brilliant white of the clouds, and took the time to feel the wind soothe his face. To Jack it felt more like hello than good-bye.

He smiled at everyone as he walked down the long corridor to Joseph's room. Walking in he saw that Joseph was asleep, but he stirred as he heard Jack. Jack took his hand and whispered, "It's okay Joseph, go back to sleep. I'm going to sit here until you wake up." Joseph smiled and slipped back into sleep. Jack sat down on the plastic chair, still holding his hand. Closing his eyes too, Jack did exactly what Simon and Sheldon had told him to do.

He couldn't tell if his eyes were open or closed. The black engulfed him. At first, he was frightened. Then a calmness he had never felt settled over him. He eased into the feeling. Then seeing a light like a sparkler lit on a dark July night in front of him, he gently walked toward it...

Asta

When I first thought of writing about the most important day of my life, I thought of when I gave birth to each of my three daughters. In my case, it took six years and lots of tests to have our first baby. In giving it more thought, I believe every mother would consider this their most meaningful day.

I then thought of the day I moved to New York, at age eighteen to start a career and live on my own. There are enough adventures in that trip to fill a book. Reaching midlife, I have so many memories, some fantastic, some not so good, but all are important to me.

Having said all of that, the memory I decided to write about is the day I answered an ad in the classified section of the Sacramento Bee, that read, "Puppies for Sale, Siberian Husky-Samoyed mix."

At the time, thirty-three years ago, my husband and I had only been married about six months when we both decided we needed a dog. The lady said she had only one female left and that she was ten dollars. That was the night Asta came into our lives and into our hearts, where she remained for sixteen years. Asta was beautiful. The perfect blend of two breeds she looked a bit like a Malamute only a lot fuzzier. She was always smiling and so much fun.

Asta was not a dog. It's just as simple as that. Asta was my friend. When she was a puppy, we took her everywhere with us. Even to the grocery store where she rode in the child's seat. No one ever asked us to leave!

On the few occasions that she could not accompany us, she stayed in her own room. At the time we were living in the house of the first doctor in Sacramento. A classic old Delta Style Victorian that had a huge panty off the kitchen with a window overlooking the back yard. This was Asta's room, decorated with framed pictures of other canine friends. We would always give her a treat when we had to leave her. A treat she would not eat until we got home.

Asta was very strong willed. Being out first baby, she did pretty much as she pleased. Like the night she ate all our cheese as well as our last ten-dollar bill. She then proceeded to throw up bits and pieces of the bill, but not enough to piece back together.

She also enjoyed a cocktail or two. We had to remind our guests to watch their drinks. Asta would drink almost anything, but she did prefer Guinness Stout or good French Champagne. Asta had taste.

Around the time Asta was two years old, my Mother died. My husband would leave for work leaving Asta and I to "chat". She was the best listener I've ever known. I don't know how I would have gotten through that heartbreaking time without Asta and her unconditional love.

Four years later we had our first daughter. A lot of our friends wondered how Asta would be with a "new baby" in the house. There was no need for worry. Asta loved the baby. She would nudge Esme's blanket over her with her nose when Esme became uncovered. When we'd all go to the park, Asta would walk alongside the stroller protecting her baby. When Jillian came along, two years later, Asta showed her the same love and affection.

By the time we moved from Texas to a little town called Galena in Maryland, Asta was 11 and slowing down a little. We moved to a 360-acre spinach farm that we loved. The girls would take Asta for long walks in the cornfield.

Later, we got the girls Flicka, a Welsh pony. Asta loved to walk Flicka on a lead and hike to the beaver pond. A very long hike for Asta, yet she always came along.

When Asta was 15, I found out I was expecting our third daughter, Nicole. Asta was okay with it. Ready to have one more to love and help with. She was always there for me when I needed her.

When I was 17, a song came out called "Mr. Bojangles" by Jerry Jeff Walker. One of the lines said, "His dog up and died. He up and died. After twenty years he still grieves". I remember thinking, "How can someone grieve 20 years for a dog who died of old age?" Those lines came back to me the day Asta died at 16 years of age.

It's now been 27 years since she left to go on before me. Her picture still hangs on the refrigerator. Every Christmas, at some time during the season, my husband will say, "I miss Asta, Asta with a big red bow around her neck on Christmas morning "sharing" a sip of eggnog and smiling." Needless to say, I miss her too. To go Jerry Jeff Walker one better, I'd have to say, "I will miss Asta till the day I die…"

Michelle

I never met Michelle, my Aunt's niece. My Aunt
Charlsie had always seemed strange to me. Almost scary at
times. Prone to snap at you, and often say things that, well,
just didn't make sense. Since she and my Uncle Tommy lived
in Texas and we lived in New York, we rarely saw one another.

It was many years later, that my Uncle Tommy found
me via the Internet. I was shocked and amazed. I had assumed
that he and my Aunt had died. As it turned out, my Aunt had
died four years before his call. I knew that my dad and Uncle
Tommy had had a falling out long ago and had never mended
things, my dad died before ever telling me what the rift had
been about. Now that Uncle Tommy was getting older, he had
wanted to find me, and reconnect.

At the time we were living in Texas. We had moved
from Maryland to be closer to my husband's family. As it
turned out, we were living less than two hours away from each
other, which is saying a lot for Texas. I couldn't wait to see him
again and to have him meet my family. Uncle Tommy was also
excited to see me again and to meet my husband and three
daughters.

Uncle Tommy was a wonderful gentle man. They don't
make them like him anymore. He was a very snappy dresser,
like my Dad, and quite the ladies' man even in his late
seventies.

We spent three amazing years together after our initial
meeting. He died in my arms, with me urging him to let go. I
told him I would be all right and we would meet again. I asked
him to give my love to everyone.

I managed to pull myself together and care for those
around me. But in all truth, I was never quite the same, never
quite myself again. Maybe having someone die in your arms,
urging them to go home, changes you in a way that can't be
expressed in words. With the strength of carrying on, comes
the fragile pain of holding onto a life that you don't understand

any more. Where did all the caretakers go? Where did all the ones with more wisdom vanish to.

So, on the day the call came that told me Michelle was sick, maybe dying in Arkansas, I knew I had to go to her. My Uncle, if he were alive, would have said, "Darlin go and see what you can do." Taking two of my three daughters, We boarded a plane for Conway Arkansas. I had no idea what lay before us.

I rented a car at the airport and drove to Michelle's house. The hospice nurse, Tracy, answered our knock. She brought us in to a house that can only be described as sparse. It was almost void of furniture and what furniture existed was of a Goodwill type. In the middle of the living room was a hospital bed with a woman lying on it. A white plastic outdoor chair was pulled up next to it. Michelle was maybe eight or so years my senior but ill health had taken its toll. Robbed her of even looking of this world. Instead she appeared more of an abandoned vehicle. An unclaimed car in a junkyard, her parts already turning to rust.

Tracy the nurse said, "Look Michelle, Cherie is here to see you." She motioned for me to come closer. It was immediately evident to me that Michelle would not be responding. Her days of speaking were long gone. I felt very uncomfortable as I looked at her.

Hesitantly, I took her hand and said, "Hello Michelle, I'm your cousin." My words fell on deaf ears. Michelle did not move. She seemed to be in a coma. I'm sure that even if she had been awake and coherent, she would not have known who I was. I had only found out that she existed about four months earlier.

Tracy never missed a beat. She introduced my daughters and chatted away as though we were seated at a table having tea. It was quite an unnerving group, my daughters looking to me for guidance on how to respond.

I explained to Tracy that we had just arrived. I thought it would be best to check into a hotel, get settled, and then return. Tracy said she'd be waiting. My daughters and I said goodbye to Michelle, who still had not opened her eyes, and we left.

After getting our things settled, we freshened up and drove back to Michelle's house. Nothing had changed in our absence. I took Tracy into the kitchen, bare, without so much as a table. She explained that she had been caring for my cousin for several months. But her health was deteriorating, she wanted family (me) to become involved, as there was a great deal of money at stake when Michelle passed away.

I knew nothing of this. My Uncle did occasionally speak about my Aunt Charlsie's sister, describing her as being more than slightly eccentric. He had told me that she lived like a bag lady. Eating leftovers in hospital cafeterias, consuming large amounts of samples at different grocery stores, and eating from trash cans. She was believed to have a tiny shack, down a long dirt road, where she lived.

Michelle had only been mentioned once. My Uncle had shown me a photograph of my Aunt Charlsie and her sister Lois taken many years ago in Mexico. In the black and white picture was a young girl, with long dark plaits, around eight years old, who stared somewhat defiantly into the camera. When I asked Uncle Tommy about her he said, "That's Michelle." That was the end of it. I didn't press the issue thinking that she had died or been estranged from the family.

Tracy also told me that a woman at the bank wished to speak with me. Since it was growing late, my daughters and I left, after telling Michelle and Tracy we would see them tomorrow. When we got back to the hotel, I phoned the woman at the bank. She asked me if I would come to see her in the morning. We arranged to meet. It had been a very exhausting day, physically and emotionally.

The next morning, I called Tracy to check on Michelle. As I expected, her condition had not changed. On the way to the bank, I was wondering if she would do better in a nursing home.

Mrs. Brown was a sharp woman, physically and mentally. She led us to her office where she immediately began to explain Michelle and her mother Lois to us.

Lois had passed away three years earlier. The entire town had been aware of her and her strange behavior. As it turned out, she was considered even more odd since everyone knew she was a millionaire. Michelle was the sole inheritor of her mother's estate. Mrs. Brown was telling me that, in the event of Michelle's death, I would become the next in line to the estate.

This took me aback. I had come solely to check on the welfare of my Uncle Tommy's niece. Instead it now felt like I was circling over her like a vulture, waiting. I was most uncomfortable with this turn of events. After telling her I would help in any way I could, I left to go and see Michelle again.

Michelle was lying just the way she had been the day before. Tracy said she had not moved during the night. Once again, we ended up in the kitchen. I asked if she didn't feel that Michelle should be in a nursing home. She said maybe soon. For now, she was content to look after her.

Staying at Michelle's house seemed pointless. Like sitting in a room waiting for a doll to suddenly wake up. We left and returned to the bank to ask who oversaw Lois's affairs. We were directed to Jill J. She told us all she knew about my aunt's sister. She then drove us, in a downpour, to Lois's house. The house was indeed a very small shack down a long winding road in the middle of what appeared to be a forest.

The house was unlivable. I don't think it had ever seen running water or an electric light. It was furnished with items that looked as though they belonged to another era. Since there was not much to be gleaned from the house, and with the rain showing no signs of letting up, we returned to Jill's car. She told us more of Lois and Michelle. Mother and daughter had apparently had a" falling out", years ago. They never spoke. Jill confirmed that Michelle seemed to suffer from mental issues, as did Lois.

Michelle called the police almost nightly, complaining about things or people that didn't exist. The police referred to her as "the girl who cried wolf." Alone in her empty house she perhaps sought out friendship or company in those not seen by others, while her mother shied away from everyone. Dressed in her many layers of clothing, even in the summer heat; she kept others at a distance preferring to exist in her own world. Mother and daughter did not take enjoyment in one another's company. Preferring to drown in shadows no one else could see.

After two day of searching for answers that would not come and looking for clues that avoided me. I felt at a total loss. What was I looking for? I was beginning to wonder what we were doing in Arkansas. How much longer did I want to keep my daughters here? It was all feeling so pointless. My Nancy Drew skills were failing me.

The next morning, I called Tracy to check on Michelle before I left to hunt down more clues. Tracy answered immediately and said, "I was just going to phone you. Michelle died moments ago. What should I do?"

We reached Michelle's house just as her body was being wheeled into an ambulance. My youngest daughter, just fifteen, started to cry. I too felt like crying. Not so much for Michelle but because the shell I was looking at was that of a life not lived. Michelle had gone through the day in day out motions of living without once feeling the magic of it all.

Tracy came out of the house holding a rather small box that contained Michelle's more important belongings, journals. Tracy wanted me to have them. I took the box and told Tracy that I would make all funeral arrangements. I thanked her for all that she had done and told her I would be in touch.

The next few days were a blur of decisions and arrangements. Michelle had almost no personal belonging. Because we found nothing, we thought appropriate for a funeral, my daughters and I bought a very nice outfit for

Michelle. We also chose a lovely necklace to complement the dress.

At the funeral parlor, the director took us to a room filled with coffins in all sizes and colors. Some even had pillows with embroidered sayings on them, such as "Rest in Peace". We chose a lovely dark wood casket with beautiful satin bedding and a pillow edged in lace. Funeral parlors are very strange places. Everyone speaking in hushed tones.

At the florist we selected a large spray of beautiful roses. The arrangement had a canvas ribbon inscribed with Psalms 23. The pastor, recommended by Tracy, said he would read Psalm 23 at the gravesite. Everything seemed to be falling into place.

A few days later we were following a hearse to a beautiful cemetery in the middle of nowhere. What a beautiful peaceful place. The same cemetery where my Aunt Charlsie and Uncle Tommy are buried as well as Michelle's mother Lois.

Months ago, I had been happy to be adding my Uncle to my dwindling family. Now I had lost another member of my Uncle's family. This one too, was permanent. A cousin I hadn't known existed and another aunt who had died before I had ever met her...

Schwarz

So many shades of black, too many to count.
I fall into the darkest of the dark.
I can, and do, disappear into shadows.
Hidden, a part of them, engulfed.
My life has always been as black as my shade.
Abandoned at an early age, I have always been on my own.
I know of nothing else.
I can, and do, fend for myself.
I expect no help, food, or affection from anyone.
I live because I am capable of caring for myself.
I am alone.

This night was unusually light. The moon slipped in
and out of the clouds. Dark one minute, brilliant the next. As
if someone were flashing a torch on and off. The old wood
buildings looked bleak, desolate in the night. Lights
occasionally swept over the grounds of the old buildings. A
lighthouse lost at sea. Still, to me it represented cover, shelter.

I slowly and cautiously made my way under the tall
wire fence. A sickening stench all about the place immediately
sickened me. Not somewhere I'd want to stay for long. For
tonight, it would do. I crouched under a loose board and found
myself in a room full of humans. Something I never seek out. I
learned long ago about humans, and how to avoid them.

The room was full to overflowing with them, all ages,
sizes, and shapes. I hugged a dusty dark corner, blending into
the void. Silent, I sat back on my haunches and watched.
Mothers trying to comfort small children. Older humans lay on
filthy mattresses. The place was cold, but still warmer than
outside. I could see snow falling through the holes in the
boards.

I shivered. It was cold but it wasn't the cold that made me
shiver. There was a very real and present evil. An evil
reflected in the hopeless black pools of the human's eyes.

I looked another way, in time to see a dark-haired little girl. She had noticed me and was silently walking towards me. She looked like she was trying to smile. I slinked away before she could get any closer. I stayed in the veil of the shadows, my ribs rubbing against the boards. Slowly, very slowly, I moved on.

I stopped in a corner. My back pressed as hard against the walls as I could stand. Much like these humans, I had no fat to protect my bones. I felt the full impact of the pain from pushing too hard. I craved, needed, the darkness. I did not want to be detected again.

I watched with eyes eager to know more. Where was I. All the sad, lonely, scared humans in one place filled me with dread and fear. I needed to leave, to be back outside. Yes, it would be cold, but it would also be safer. I wanted to be alone, on my own. This place did not meet my needs.

I had started looking for a way out, when I saw it, a streak of gray. Not a big streak but still food. Instinct took over and I left the shadows, my safe place, to pounce. I hadn't eaten for a day or two. Hunger made the kill. I spent no time toying. I simply killed and ate. I went unnoticed as I went back to the wall to wash and watch.

The room was silent with sounds of moaning and humans sleeping. Small humans cried. The bigger humans had given up and simply lay there and let the small humans cry themselves to sleep: crying of hunger, crying of cold, crying of fear, crying of the unknown. There was no comfort to give. The air held its breath.

I must have dozed off, not full but no longer as hungry as before. I awoke, to a loud flash of bright cruel light as doors were sprung open. Exposing a cover of white with a chill that surpassed that of the room. We all shivered, a moving mass of filth hardened by the cold, stiff, unsure. Orders to stand and come forward out to the white, out to the cold, were shouted into the room. Hitting the walls hard with their brutal assault. Some had just fallen asleep and were now being summoned out into the vast white. The humans stood and followed; blank, feet walking nothing more, flesh shuffling on wood.

I thought, "Now is the time to leave, now is the time to escape." But somehow, I felt this wasn't finished. I knew nothing of what was happening here. A strange unusual feeling crept over me. I wanted to know more, to know why. I felt torn. Afraid to stay, afraid to leave.

I crept back into the shadow hugging the wall, watching, and waiting. I didn't wait for long. The wood doors slammed open. Humans sliding in, some, not all, the space less crowded. Cold, bare, lifeless with all the humans spilling in, still lifeless.

I took a chance to get to the doors before they shut again but I was too late. They were closing as I came near. There was a large metal trashcan by the door. Maggots were moving in it. Again, my hunger took over and I ate my fill. No eye fell on me. I was invisible as always.

I was frightened. It smelled of death. It was all around. We were swallowed by it. Drowning in it. I longed to fill my lungs with fresh air no matter how cold. To make a fresh kill, to eat, sleep, to be alone. Looking around I saw nothing, no opening. Trapped.

So, this is how it feels to be toyed with. For me the feeling was familiar. Only now I was the victim. Again, I was scared. Shivering I went to look for somewhere out of sight. Somewhere I could be alone. Stay awake and watch.

There were beds stacked one on top of another. One far against a wall was dark. I melted under it, waiting, watching and listening. Full, I wanted to sleep but fear, an overwhelming fear, kept me awake. I curled into a tight ball, trying to disappear. I wanted out desperately. The crying, the moaning was starting again. Comfort, only a word. Total desolation was all there was. The dank darkness engulfed me, almost suffocating, with the dust and filth I was curled in.

Trapped I stayed as still as possible. Waiting and longing for my chance, my opportunity to escape. The darkness was coming. Closing us, sealing us in for the night. I stayed still, afraid to move, afraid not to. There was no getting out tonight. The doors sealed tight; the holes too small.

I tightened myself into an even tighter ball. Sleep would not join me tonight. The small humans never stopped crying. Until suddenly they just went quiet. Perhaps sleep took pity on them and for a few brief hours took them away with dreams of happier times. Sleep did not refuse them.

My need to get away became overwhelming. I slowly made my way to the doors, the only way in or out. They would open again. I would be ready. I crouched close to the wall. But this time in a position that I could spring from, the second the doors slammed open. I waited. I didn't have long to wait.

The strong heavy doors flung open, as quickly as they had shut just hours ago. Two men in dark uniforms flashed torches around the horror of the room. No one dared look. No one dared breathe. I alone jumped to my feet and flew out the doors. Running as I have never run before, running from the stench, the cold, the humans who were now only lost souls waiting, running for my life.

I was almost to the fence when I heard the humans laughing and then the loud crack. The whirring of the metal as it flew past my right ear. I kept running. Nothing could make me stop. Again, and again I heard the loud crack. But by now I was safe. I was in the heart of the blackness of the forest, my friend.

I stopped to catch my breath. I was thankful to be free of that evil dark place. Thankful to be alive, free of the humans, and free to live. It was then that I felt the sharp sting of my ear. Saw the black redness that fell onto the white snow at my feet.

Tentatively I took my paw and very slowly, very gently, felt my ear. It no longer went to a point at the end. Instead it now was a slanted tear. I lay my head on the snow, the coldness numbing the pain. After a while the bleeding stopped. It would heal. I would carry it with me always, a reminder. A reminder I did not need to carry in the flesh.

The night in that building of evil, has never left me. It would be with me always. I would wake often from dreams thinking I was back there, trapped. I still, and always will, avoid humans. They are a stupid arrogant lot in my opinion, able to turn untrustworthy and frightening in a heartbeat. As in all things, some may be good. I've yet to find any who are. Then again, I keep to myself, more now than before.

I have heard the humans say I have nine lives. I know I used one that night. By keeping to myself, by being on my own, I believe I will be able to keep my other eight...